Fire

in

the

Hole

Fire in the Hole

stories

KRISTIE BETTS LETTER

Engine Books
Indianapolis

Engine Books
Indianapolis, IN
enginebooks.org

Also available in eBook formats from Engine Books.

10 9 8 7 6 5 4 3 2 1

ISBN: 978-1-938126-76-5

Library of Congress Control Number: 2019952875

For Mary and Maddy

My guide and I entered that hidden road
to make our way back up to the bright world.
We never thought of resting while we climbed.
                         —Dante Alighieri, *The Inferno*

Well now everything dies baby that's a fact
But maybe everything that dies someday comes back.
Put your makeup on, fix your face up pretty
And meet me tonight in Atlantic City.
                         —Bruce Springsteen, "Atlantic City"

CONTENTS

Silver Cornet Band

BANDS, 1872

Shimmering gray in the sky. The cold air tastes like metal, even though you're pulling through thousands of trees. "At least there's no lightning now, Miss," the driver says. "The Rockies are so close to the sky that fire just jumps right down." The ridge road torn from the mountainside barely keeps the stage upright. On the left side of the narrow road, the rocky ground plummets; only a few scrubby pines would stop your fall.

Keep your eyes up.

When the wind blows, be sure to hold onto something. Several fellows were swept clean off the mountain, they told you in Central City. When you get to Caribou, a bowl of land curves beneath three hills. Atop the hills, the land opens into eight mine mouths, while rough buildings and straight roads quilt the valley.

The tossing coach stops in the center of the fresh town. At a Denver parade, you met a man playing in the Caribou Silver Cornet Band, a man who cobbled shoes for miners. Harvey Eben, a religious man, had a lung condition-which-was-almost-consumption, characterized by breathless attacks, kept him in the clear dry air. The dark thick mineshaft would have been the death of him. Yet he fit metal nails into boots in a in a high-elevation boomtown lit by near-constant lightning he took to be judgment. He chose you.

The ring of course is silver, though you hoped for gold.

"Well, dear, what to you imagine God will bless us with?" Harvey asks the morning after.

"Could we get a cow here?" you ask.

He laughs. "My bride fancies a cow as a wedding gift."

The dogs stalk around Caribou, all scrappy, all with extra-thick fur. They're hearty, loud, seemingly indestructible except for those two mutts who get struck by lightning mid-mating. The preacher tries convincing people to disentangle the charred remains before burial, but no one's willing. The lucky families with cows also have small barns. Harvey's cabin (your cabin) just has the one room, the one building.

Harvey tells you about the Thompsons, who were used to Virginia winters where a roof overhang is plenty for livestock. Here, during the winter, they had to bring the cow into their cabin, much to Mrs. Thompson's horror. The poor creature kept getting its nose frozen to the ground. Mrs. Thompson said that living with a cow would surely be the death of her, but actually the opposite was true. The weight of snow and gales of wind were more than Mr. Thompson's carpentry could sustain. One night the roof fell in, and would have killed the five little Thompsons where they lay, but for the cow's broad back, which caught the roofbeams. The cow died heroically and the Thompsons spent the remainder of the winter living with the Spensers.

Mrs. Thompson was heard to whisper that she preferred the cow.

The cabin is small enough with your body and his. Another creature would push you that much closer together.

"Come see," he yells. It's not a cow, but it's something. Harvey trades twelve pairs of winter boots to get you (his bride) a fine young goat. Now your domestic chores include the goat, the cooking, the clothes, and the wood.

If any thunder rumbles, no matter how distant, your tall husband prays. "The Lord sends us messages," he says. "The voice of the Lord criticizing devilment."

"Then you should have nothing to worry about." You lace your boots to bring in wood for the night. Harvey murmurs each evening about the Lord's intentions for your prospective children. More nights than you can count, you fall asleep to the buzzing of Harvey's interpretation of the Lord's will.

SALVES

Who can lead a boomtown band with cracked lips? Especially if he happens to be the cornet player. The unforgiving mountain air chafes everything in its path.

You add your small things (three dresses, a set of dishes, your mother's sewing box) to Harvey Eben's household items (a Hawken pistol, a silk hat, piles of shoe leathers). The pegs, awls, and metal shapes he keeps in his corner of the general store, but he does his stitching occasionally by the fire.

His lips crack. The Silver Cornet Band is to play at Saturday's political meeting, but the cornet shines coldly in the corner as Harvey licks his wounded lips.

"You ought not lick them," you say.

"If I don't, they pain me more." Already, deeply etched lines bleed past the lipline on the left side of his mouth. He likes everything soft. How much money did he spend on that feather bed, too soft for death to land on? You guess it works, since you've suffered no fatalities yet. He says it's for your comfort, but this is a man not born to suffer. Now Harvey searches for something to keep the cracking cold from his lips. At every opportunity he rubs his mouth with the softest things he can find: the inside of sheepskin gloves, his own tongue, the rim of his grey silk hat. None of these repel the cold, the cracks. The silver cornet stays wrapped in its soft cloth, sleeping beside the fireplace. The cool metal soothes at first, but when Harvey tries to force air through the mouthpiece his lips pull away from the silver instrument in pained shock.

You don't tell him, but his face is almost comical when he tries. It puts you in mind of the goat.

You visit Van & Tabor's store in search of salve. The foul Pullman's remedy they provide gives Harvey a rash. He rages about the four cents, and you cry into the potato cakes as he melts snow to wash his face for the third time. You lace up again to take Pullman's Tonic and Restoration Elixir for Skin back to Van & Tabor's, to ask for those four cents back. Joel Van shakes his head. "We're not responsible for the elixir's failure because it simply indicates weakness in the subject. Put the Pullman's on a stronger man, Ma'am, and you won't be so disappointed."

You stare out the window at the snowglare beyond to keep your eyes busy. Joel Van has a mouth like a featherbed, neither cracked nor bleeding. A brightly dressed man who smells of a mixture of molasses and gunpowder puts a kid-gloved hand on your shoulder. "Ma'am, the Shoo Fly has all kinds of potions that could help your Harvey."

"Truly?"

"Can't ask a man nothing about skin fixes. Up there they know all about skin. Can mix you up just what you need." He smiled at Joel Van, who scowled back.

"A lady doesn't visit that type of establishment."

You ignore Joel Van and his big pink mouth.

The directions are to a house on the east side of town behind the Shoo Fly Saloon, and you've been to church with Harvey enough to know where the church-going wives point their fingers. But you go ahead and knock on the whorehouse door. You smile at the pretty girl with flyaway hair who opens it. You feel the full weight of your heavy wool dress, and the fat weight of your own tongue behind teeth.

"Well, honey, why so glum?" the woman asks.

"I'm Melinda Eben, Mrs. Eben. My Harvey sews the shoes."

"And plays a mean cornet, if I recall." The woman slides a brush through her waist-length hair. "I saw him play at the Sherman House on the Fourth of July."

"Was that right before the big lightning storm?"

"That's the one. We lost the first Shoo Fly when the lightning struck. That dark skeleton next door is all that's left."

"All this lightning scares me."

You don't even realize you are twisting your ring. The girl nods. "Sweetheart, don't touch silver when storms are about. You know the lightning just lingers in the air here. It likes shiny things, just like the magpies."

You sink into a velvet chair, and your scalp tingles with conversation. Once the tongue problem subsides, you discuss dry skin, flyaway hair, chapped lips, and other intimacies. You leave with a honey salve to mix with goat's milk each evening. The girl with the flyaway hair promises the elixir will soften Harvey's lips and make him smell better. It does both. The lotion smells like the buzzing fields of summer, warm and lovely.

ROPES

Mornings crackle. Ice moves on the roofboards and distant trees. Air too cold wakes Harvey with chest constrictions, seizing his lungs. At the first rasp, you pull yourself into the cold, waking and put a pot of water on the stove. You blow into the stove slightly to hurry the water's boil. Harvey's breath whistles.

"Here, it's beginning to steam."

Like a drowning man, Harvey inhales deeply. He coughs, and the steam soothes his chest. You pat his back, watching shiny droplets form on his brow, as his eyes close with the drugged satisfaction of the deep breath.

Your second year as wife.

"The snow must stop." Your husband evaluates the quality of light coming in through the opaque leathers drawn tight across the cabin's one window. "They'll have to shut down the mines if this weather doesn't let up. Pray for sun."

Perhaps because you don't pray, the winds rise at midday. Whether or not fresh snow falls, no one in Caribou knows, because the howling swirls of snow could be coming from either the drifts or the sky. The miners and workingmen can't lift their eyes into the stinging snow. The Caribou Mine dug a protective walkway, which although half caved-in, has the essential logs marking its passage. Banging ankles against the lines of frozen logs, the men make their way to the mouth of the mine.

Returning that evening is the problem. They path goes only halfway down Idaho Street, barely to the center of town, and beyond that nothing but blind white. Most of the Moyles, Tom Little, and Caleb Dotterson can clamber across the snowcrust to their adjacent cabins. Others bunk with neighbors, or in the places of business on Idaho Street.

For the rest, there are ropes.

In the hard-packed piles covering the first floor windows of the Sherman House, ropes lead to the lights of the warm second story. Many miners mumble "coffee" and begin to ascend. Seventeen faint ladies wait on the other end, leaning quickly out of window frames for a final hand up.

How many miners climb the frozen drifts, holding onto the ropes unfurled by princesses above? Where do they sleep, and whose husbands are they? How do the ladies know to leave the Shoo Fly Saloon and head up from the outskirts? Werely's Saloon hosts more refugees from the Seven Thirty, the No Name, and the Poorman. When the swirling snow settles, as tall as a full-grown tree in several drifts, most miners come out broke, and the public houses of Idaho Street have empty cabinets and full coffers. No one talks about it. The sun breaks through on the first of December and the other Caribou wives renew their ties with their husbands.

Weather comes before questions.

You hear that the static electricity inside the Sherman House lit the night. Bodies warmed up with wool socks and each other flashed lights so bright that many a wife swore she saw lightning coming from her snowbound husband's general direction.

Later, William Donald will act befuddled as to how his second floor filled with the Shoo Fly's faint ladies. "Nothing wrong with reading the weather," a whore is said to have responded.

But Harvey is not one of the men in the golden entrapment. Harvey never makes it to his cobbler corner of the general store. He's not a brave man, and he turns back before he gets to the corner by the Dillinger barn. He does not have to join the other men in the second story. Although everyone exclaims at your good fortune for having a husband home, you notice just how little space or fresh air the cabin offers. Harvey has too little work to keep him busy on normal days, much less while snowbound at home.

One week without leaving the room, one week with the smell of the bucket, one week with the proximities of marriage. You wish he were one of the men with ropes.

After that week, superstitions buzz, about boots, about weather. Three men return shoes in the space of four days. The boots, secured with the metal nails, made to transition from the bitter drifts to the cold muds of spring, have been making men feel weak. Especially when the nails come in contact with raw earth on those electric days before storms. These men whisper about Harvey, about shoes. Nonetheless, watertight boots are as necessary as bread. So mostly everyone mutters over boots and chats about the Lord. Even Harvey's fervor for God dulls with constant mention.

"Everyone is calling upon the Lord these days," he says, following up with a dubious "Praise be."

"Especially when they pick up boots."

The early spring wind dismantles the corners of Caribou. The roof flies from the Donaldson's boarding house, a tree blows into the sorting room of the Poorman mine, and an unhitched wagon crashes through the church doors. Moses Mosley's underfed horse disappears one Sunday afternoon while tied outside of Werley's saloon. Moses swears up and down that the wind took the horse, post and all. His brothers agree, but say that any horse with a bellyful of oats couldn't be swept away, even by the Rocky Mountain wind. Three fires bloom on Caribou Hill after a storm.

"Lightning walks among us," you say. "Caribou is a lightning town."

"That's preposterous," Harvey replies redoing the button on his left sleeve. "You feel the presence of the Lord, the Almighty God. I heard him speak the other day as I was walking into town."

"Listen: that crackling in the air. Something is going to burst into flames any moment."

"That is devil talk. Fetch my salve." The lines of his face do not make your heart flutter. Your pride at saving the Silver Cornet Band and keeping your husband's lips supple becomes less glorious each evening as you watched Harvey slather his mouth with sap and goat's milk.

In the hands of a more graceful man, it could be lovely.

STRIKES

The Mining Company Nederland, doing business from the other side of the Atlantic, squeezes more out of thin air. Without working capital, the Dutch persist in working the mines without improvements. To the miners, they offer paltry wages, deteriorating conditions and the spook of ghost ownership.

Suspicions run high as to which miners and mines worked for whom and which veins attach to which mine mouths after three lodes intersected somewhere deep beneath Caribou Hill. You think it all must connect beneath. The separate lodes vein together into a tumbling silver jumble somewhere underground. The kid-gloved gentry that sometimes rides in, stepping away from the mountain stage as if wounded by its roughness, produces documents and gives speeches to groups of tired men who spend each spring day removing as much water from mineshafts as they do blasting the silver that pays salaries.

Harvey's business fares poorly. The miners have less money, but they also become suspicious of Harvey's shoemaking. Several more men report being overtaken by a tingling weakness when wearing the sturdy hobnailed boots. Rumors swirl that Harvey allows spirits into the shoes.

He tells you to pray.

You see the flyaway faint lady out gathering flowers, and you're glad. You sit on a rock and talk for the better part of an hour. She tells you what everyone else won't. "They say he pays the Tommy Knockers in trinkets to cobble those shoes each night. Most miners won't put on a pair of Harvey's shoes without rubbing salt inside and saying a prayer." Now you know.

You laugh, not at the superstition, but at the idea that

Harvey would be on intimate terms with Tommy Knockers. "Why, any kind of Tommy Knocker would send my husband into convulsions," you say.

The springtime wet inspires lightning. You begin to think that lightning waits in the ground, wanting to travel back up into the sky if it doesn't find any fires to start.

Still, can't blame boots for weather.

Despite the salve, Harvey leaves the cornet shrouded in the corner, and the Silver Cornet Band hasn't played since the Fourth of July. Without the instrument, what's left?

The goat gets struck. Its milk has softened Harvey's lips and your hair. Plus, you like the creature with its soft fur and devilish eyes. But it's the same storm from the south that knocks Merle Richards clean off his crutches. While Merle gets up, he says that his knee feels better but his ears are ringing. That is exactly when the little gray goat just curls up and dies. You hear the creature's crackling scattering of final sounds.

"The lightning got our goat, Harvey," you say when your husband walks in and sets down his lunch pail.

Harvey unthreads his kneeboots. Lace by lace. "We must pray all evening. This is a message from the Lord that we have cracks, letting the sin in, Melinda." He glares at you. Then shivers.

"Didn't you hear about Merle Sanders? This is not a message, Harvey. This town is too high up, too much a wind-drop. Can we please leave here?"

"God was just giving Merle a small message about his drinking, and praise be his knee seems better. A sort of miracle. The Lord has His ways, Melinda."

"The Lord did not kill our goat."

"You cannot presume to know what He intends! I felt the

presence of the Lord this afternoon…"

"No, No, No. You felt the lightning. That was not God, that was cloudfire." Your words on the air surprise you.

"I'll not have this conversation."

"You'll also not have your salve! That goat protected your Godly instrument. But you know I can go down to the Shoo Fly and get some salve. Those nice ladies know all about lip softener. Let me just get on my shoes."

"You'll not leave this house." He pushes you into place before he begins to wind the laces back up his boot. You wait until he leaves before you cry.

BANDS, 1875

After Harvey returns to town, you move around the cabin without anything to take your attention. A sound outside rings strong and musical—Harvey playing his cornet in a conciliatory gesture? But no. The frenzied song is wind, returning from the Continental Divide.

With the last fingerfuls of the honey salve, you coat your own papery lips and manage to work your wedding ring free. You set the silver ring in the center of the pine table—a charm against being followed by lightning—and put on your old leather boots.

The wind slaps the door closed behind you. If you grip bonnet in one hand and the left side of your dress in the other, your feet are free to run. A sharp wail of air thundering across the slope. Your skirt catches the current, pushes you further. Stay close to the buildings.

You know how not to be struck.

Tally

Toto

Beach town, off-season, a few faded holiday decorations blow in the sandy breeze. Two middle-aged figures walk towards each other on the boardwalk.

TALLY: Toto?

(*A flash of recognition, corresponding intake of breath. Beneath the adult, a flash of eyelashes, of the familiar.*)

TOTO: Oh, hey.

(*Eyes widen, lips part, hips remember. A darkness lit by long planes. When hands trembled, when everything trembled.*)

TALLY: Long time no see.

(*A memory of then, of the press, of the wideness. Of that one time on the rooftop, or when they were so entwined the smallest wave almost sent them over. Breath vibrates, buzzes, bee-like.*)

TOTO: It's been a while.

(*The pressure, the constant touching. To return to that was a return to body, to hunger, to a time before pajamas.*)

TALLY: This place is the same.

(*Sand, faded boardwalk, seagull screams. Once those sounds and sights melted on her skin. Smaller and sadder now.*)

TOTO: Yeah, that's the thing about tourist towns. Nice to see you.

(*All of it: the everything, the didn't, the breathlessness then, now just breathing.*)

TALLY: Yes.

(*Beneath this serious flesh, the ghost of all desire.*)

They continue walking.

Late July,

Clover Lick,

West Virginia

"Stay back," one boy said when he saw the shape circling.

But then they moved closer. The two boys laid their t-shirts near a red rock.

One boy's shoulders matted with freckles, the other's skin steady brown but for three pink mosquito bites.

The blond boy would one day grow lots of hair to protect his pink skin, but not yet. Summer buzzed and leaked from the wide leaves above them. The river steamed. Overabundant life.

"What is it?"

"Don't ask."

A white mound swirled in the mudded water. The shirtless boys stepped onto the mossy rocks rising out the river.

"Is it a fish?"

The boy was close enough to know that slowly spinning curve was certainly not a fish. The body held onto water and the exposed stomach plumped like overripe fruit. The boys stared and stirred the water with a stick. Then poked. Then they laid their hands on top of the stretched stomach. Silent. Reverent.

"It's kind of beautiful," one finally said.

"Yes." They pressed their shoulders together.

When the afternoon outlines dissolved in early evening, they pulled their t-shirts over clammy thin chests. One boy got slapped with the perforated end of a belt for being late and smelling bad. Three days later the other boy moved to

Alamagordo, New Mexico.

There is no such thing as a full inoculation, but neither boy felt a certain kind of fear again.

Alien

Ears

I only see ghosts when I've been drinking.

Maybe the liquor helps me believe, or maybe edges need to go softer. Mostly the dark shapes cluster around my son. Now he is six, and sometimes chats with them.

I'd like to dry up a bit, but after pouring drinks all night I need one.

When the boy was a baby I felt sure these shadows surrounding him, humming tunelessly, were evil spirits—here to punish me for drinking on the job. But now when I sneak up on him, the conversations are pleasant and make him giggle. Only when I drink a few beers at the end of my shift, out with the girls, or a few glasses of wine with my sister at home—then the corners of my eyes fill. Slow moving shapes, shadows. Nothing substantial, no recognizable relatives.

My husband never sees anything, and never wants to hear about it. My attempt to pinpoint a particular one in the corner of the kitchen failed. Also they don't seem to come around much when he's home. Recently he's been driving to Ohio for weeks at a time, and as soon as he leaves, my son's little conversations start. I ask, "Who are you talking to?" My boy just says, "Anyone."

Either we both have the same hauntings, or we both make up people to fill up space.

•

"Amaretto Sour, please." A man with soft hands settled on the stool. Smiled at me. I smiled back, but wanted to tell him to keep his voice down. To order a beer or a Jim Beam. To sit further away from the cowboy-swagger regulars.

"Are you working down at the observatory?" I asked. Crisply dressed fellows came to Green Bank, West Virginia only for the National Radio Astronomy Observatory or because they were lost on their way to a ski resort.

"How did you guess?" he asked, looking momentarily bemused.

"We don't get many types here." The man lapped his Amaretto Sour delicately and crossed his legs. He was the only person in the Dairy Bar not wearing boots. "Your shirt is pink. And ironed."

"Yes, yes. Right on both counts, although I believe the catalogue promised 'salmon.'"

"So what do you do at the observatory?" Everyone else with their pool sticks and cigarettes—cartoon shapes, familiar. No shadows. I wiped this wooden bar each night, bailing out a boat with an unstoppable leak.

"I listen. I work in the scientific field of listening."

I put down my pink rag and leaned in.

No one can believe that cell phones don't work in Green Bank. Everyone thinks you're making one of those West Virginia jokes about brothers chasing their sisters.

No joke.

All reception, except for the big stuff, is gone. We all still have land-lines, and I imagine my aunt in Brooklyn would laugh and laugh.

He told me he was in town for a week, doing an operations check at the NRAO to try to hear what the others had missed.

Reviewing tapes, new signals, patterns in computer bleeps. In the bar, without a phone for companionship, he tilted his head towards me.

"Are you listening for aliens?" I asked. Growing up in Green Bank, I heard so many rumors about the cross-planetary communication. The government kept secrets because the aliens were running elections and building us weapons. The satellites really spied on Communists in space. The aliens were telling us cancer cures, we didn't want other countries to know. Whatever the reason, officials had squirreled away a listening station in a place without two lane roads. Why else would anyone build a Radio Observatory in the middle of the Appalachian Mountains? And not even on the top of one for better reception? Only one radio station came in, from Charleston, with another fuzzy one from Staunton on clear days. Two radio stations don't suggest great reception. Expensively exotic bowls tipped mysteriously in the rolling hills—something secret has to be happening.

"We are listening for patterns," he said. "Alien means foreign, from another place, not just 'from Mars.' No one expects 'take us to your leader.' At least not in so many words." He peered at two men in Harley t-shirts debating a pool call, their bearded faces close enough to kiss.

"Don't worry about them," I said. "They're best buddies who always start squawking after a few beers." One of the Harley guys grabbed the other's beard, but after a tense moment the two started laughing and went outside to light each other's cigarettes.

"Do you want to hear my theory about alien abductions?" I asked.

Now the scientist leaned forward, his round belly squeezing against his pink shirt.

"It's all about babies," I said.

When I had my son I couldn't believe the lights. Hospitals must have the brightest lights of anyplace. Piercing light. Different than the sun. The light made me wonder about the poor little creature leaving a warm, dark bath for this artificial brilliance. I kept trying to tell my husband, to make sure he made shade for the baby when it arrived so it wasn't scared. But my handsome husband of four months patted my hand and guffawed at the TV mounted in the corner of the room.

"All those people who are abducted all say they see blinding light and medical stuff, right?" I said.

He nodded.

"After I had my son I read all those instruction manuals. That's how I figured it out. The book said that an infant's sight doesn't develop the same depth perception grownups have until the baby is several months old. They focus in on one thing and everything else slides away into a peripheral blur."

His nodding increased in tempo. He seemed to nod once for each word I said.

"Babies love eyes," I explained across the bar.

"So our visions of the almond-headed aliens with huge eyes are simply every baby's first impression of an alien world?" His own eyes glowed too light for his pale round face.

"Exactly," I replied.

"Brilliant. The return of the repressed."

At the end of the night, the scientist stayed as I cleaned up and drank a few amaretto sours with him. He had asked if I wanted to walk through the observatory. Lingering customers were still sinking balls; I wished he had a better sense of when to whisper.

But how was he to know that his bartender was married? I never wore my ring to work because it left a greenish stain whenever my hand was wet with alcohol. My husband had been gone for eight days, seventy-eight for the year.

The moon has no light of its own, only the borrowed

brilliance of the sun. Each of the satellite dishes was a concave copy, reflecting pale light from the real moon. The only other time I had been in the NROA field, I rode in with my best friend. Her father worked at the Observatory and that social difference got her better clothes and her own horse. She just laughed when a man in a spotted tie yelled at us from a doorway. We were untouchable. Three days after turning seventeen, she eloped with an Army sergeant. She sends me pictures every Christmas of her three—no, four now—girl children. I look carefully at the girls in matching dresses, trying to see my best friend in them. Like most people who leave the county, I doubt she plans on coming back.

Tonight the satellite field hummed with a new intensity. I held the scientist's small, soft hand in mine, and was reminded again how much I missed my best friend. My companion stopped periodically to point to the stars.

"Ursa Minor."

He pointed out the light blue barracks where he was staying—close to the satellites, so that he would not be far away if there were something to hear in the middle of the night. Farther from the reception area, with its parking lot, cafeteria and long rows of offices, the buildings disappeared. Only satellite dishes glowed. We wandered between the huge metal bowls, deceptively small and fragile from a distance, but huge whorled ears up close.

"Orion." He pointed past the satellite to the sky.

"Pleiades," he said, sweeping one arm upward with the rhythm of vowels, and then down to brush the side of my face. The lingering "s" brushed again, like an incantation, a word that turns into something as soon as it hits the air.

Then of course we bridged the distance and lay on the grass, which had only just started to cool from the August day's accumulated warmth. No words, no sounds, no distinctions between my softness and his. In the moonlight he was formless, with no angles to push me away. My husband was slashed with muscles from raising roofbeams and hammers, with big callused hands pressing. This man floated into me like a sound gathering force and crescendo. No bones beneath the pliable surface of his skin. In the reflected light of the satellite moon curving above us, we were both graceful underwater creatures.

I still felt the softening effects of alcohol as I fumbled my keys in the door. My sister snored in her room, earning her free rent with babysitting when I worked nights. I went to the back bedroom to watch my son sleep. While my sister slept loudly—mouth open, arms flung—my son slept so silently that I used to press my face against his chest to be sure of his breathing.

A sound, conversational and definitely not his gentle exhale, came from the room.

I could see him, a mound of yellow jammies, curled against the wall. Something seemed to move next to his bed. I felt my way into his room with my eyes closed, pulled up the kicked-back covers, and kissed him quickly. I did not want to look at anything. In my room undressing, I deliberately looked away from a fluttering in the hallway.

The hazy night left me wondering if we had even kissed on the lips. I couldn't remember exactly. If we didn't kiss on the lips, then certainly the act meant something other than betrayal.

For four more nights the same routine: bar then satellites, until I was sure of several things, including the kissing. Once, while we were wound together on the grass, I happened to float up above our shaky flesh and look back down. The darkened field was dotted with glowing curves, each satellite straining in a slightly different direction, and also in the humming listening field, two moon-pale bodies. A slight hill spotted with satellites, surrounded on three sides by forest. I kept floating up above the curvy land, and saw the two bodies (two only—I counted the feet) roll to the left.

That night was the final one.

Driving out of the parking lot, the radio satellites were not moons. Just large metal things pointed at the sky. Hard and cold. I tried to picture the scientist somewhere else, at the sister radio observatory in Socorro, New Mexico—the same configuration of satellites but on sand beneath a wider sky. Inside the scooped out mountain he described in Colorado Springs, full of glittering computers in a war-proof dome. Or sent out to fix one of the flying satellites circling the earth to try and catch all the sounds that don't make it down. I could not imagine his softness topped with a space helmet, or any kind of technological exoskeleton. I could not imagine him anywhere.

On the road home, one house still glowed. The TV satellite dish loomed half as large as the house. These neighbors could still get the Miss America pageant even in lousy weather. The only downside was that they had to hand-crank their dish to catch each separate band of channels. Maybe the neighbors do much more than I do to pull the world in to a small living room in this small county where nothing worth broadcasting ever happens, and all communication breaks down.

My house was noisy for this time of night. I tripped over a pair of sneakers and cursed. My sister's snoring hiccuped. On the couch again, curled up to the blue TV light.

I felt my way down the hall to check on my son. I left the TV on so as not to hear anything else.

The boy breathed wet and steady, with a shadow pressing against him. This shadow nearly covered the bed, shaded him. A hum mixed with his low serious breathing. I should close my eyes and turn away. Nothing is there. Nothing is ever there. But I walked up, took off my shoes and stepped into the shadow, laying myself across whatever was next to him. A momentary cold, and then the warm surface of my son's small back. The hum settled into the white noise of the back bedroom. I put my arm around him and closed my eyes.

Later in the night, something pulled me awake. I still had my arm draped across my sleeping son, but someone else pressed against my back. My senses woke up before my mind. Had they come back because I was in their space? My breath whinnied, and I could not make myself turn around.

"Hey." My husband pressed his hardness against me. I took in a full breath of his ghosts: cigarettes, gasoline, salt. My body sank right into him.

"Keep talking." His breathing hummed against my cheek as I reached back to hold the firm handle of his hip.

The Little

Match

Girl

You know the walls are metal, even with fake wood stapled on top, those dark lines playing at boards. The worst is when mornings bleed into afternoons. You feel that metal when you can't wake her up, because it's too thick, too early, too loud, too bright.

Don't even.

She doesn't notice you wear her almost-pink slippers. Did she notice the electric won't come on? She likes it dark so she can sleep it off. Sometimes, she wakes you up when she gets home, crashing into cabinets, banging pans around and then watches the cable. But if she stays too late, she just falls on her bed or that one time, on the bathroom floor, right on top of her sick.

On the table, her matches say Wild Nightingales, right beside a bunch of muddy quarters.

In Danish Acres, rows of aluminum boxes fill with faces like hers, eyes fogged and skin scraped rough. Only the Ethiopian family smiles, with white teeth and spines straight up. Inside theirs, only rugs and no tv at all. You wish you could be on all those rugs. Here, there hasn't been milk in forever.

The slipper skids on a catalogue full of toys, dolls and pale kids with straight shiny hair. The first match folds in half after making a spit sound.

The second stays up.

Those pretty-hair girls go purple and orange. With the glow, the walls become what was on the TV before the cable went.

Red and orange and blues and greens all in the middle of winter where the sky's another concrete floor.

Only now color's inside.

When the match blinks out, walls come back. Blotchy, not-wood. The yellow ceiling tilts. Cold corners echo her croaky breath from the bedroom.

The whole pack makes a bigger snap. You try to hold on as long you can but the party colors bite at fingers. They jump to pages to wrappers to the blanket, all edges with purple blooming red.

The walls, the dark dark walls warm with new.

More color than the mall, than that movie where some kid stays alone in a mansion at Christmas. The smell like at Gramma Pat's, back when she had a fireplace, right in the center of the room.

The glow hums but not too loud.

Not loud enough to wake her up.

No more nighttime or concrete skies or that sour smell, only bright bright bright bright bright—

The Effects

of

Global Warming

on the

Sunny Side Café

It's too hot for coffee, too dim for toast, but still. You stare out towards the harbor through the haze of ashy bits airborne, the haze of damp dinge. Beneath the blur, the surface wavers as smells crawl up from the ocean, and you want to stretch out on the cool plastic coating of the corner booth, the one with the triangular view of the harbor. Corner booths are for lovers and drug dealers escaping the heat. In the Sunny Side, thin smoke expands with what's scraped off the grill, with whine of drills and motors, with radio playing Elvis. Your arms full of napkins and salt shakers, you bend over the corner booth. A small sea lion stretches. Hunched in by way of the kitchen door propped open for deliveries. All the in-betweens, of fur and flipper, of sea and sidewalk. Of the desire to find the place where warm-not-hot spreads out without reservation. In the red press of this haze, the sinew-eared seal stares back. The booth's cool plastic frames harbor's triangle, soft pointed face, flat flippers, and black eyes of liquid loss.

Real

Estate

The best time to invest in real estate is when the market's down. That's when I got in.

They were burying Little Roy, but thinking about that hole in the ground made the space between my fingers feel like poison ivy. I left to go check out my property. I trucked across the sandy mud of Elysian Fields cemetery, still steaming from the last batch of summer rain. A few of the guys looked at me funny when I turned away, but I hardly recognized them. Back in the day we were all footballers and brawlers, but now everyone looked soft. Lots of them still had the ponytails, but no hair on top. All us guys had long hair in the 70s, but once the top goes it's time to quit.

In the church, they had played that music, the echoey kind that sounds like the mall at Christmas. If churches want folks to take mourning seriously, they need to play Hank Williams. Little Roy would have hated what they played. I hummed a little Hank.

At least when I went, I'd have Little Roy nearby. My plot was number D409 and Little Roy was only as far away as the K row.

They must have been doing some kind of groundwork. Or gardening.

My plot of land, my only real estate holding, had recently been dug up. About six feet of it. Maybe I was in the C row rather than the D row. No, I could see the small metal markers.

That rectangle of semi-sandy earth was number 409, like the cleaner. Each of the gravesites had a number so everyone could find the dearly departed. I checked, double-checked, and walked up from a new angle. It was D409.

Someone was newly buried there.

Really, who would bury someone in a random grave?

Mobsters.

Husbands who snapped and strangled their wives.

People who were ridiculous about their pets. Maybe a mangy spaniel lay curled on one of those flowery pillows. People had to be out of their socket or up to no good to steal a final resting place, that's for sure.

I had even made a speech to my boy the last time I saw him and took him to the swimming hole. "I bought some prime real estate for you, son" I said. "Are you going to swim with your t-shirt on? It'll get in the way."

"No, I like it on," Danny said, crossing his arms across the points of his flabby chest. The kid could use some swimming against the current.

"So when I kick it, you don't have to worry about a thing. Don't go for anything fancy either. Say a few words over me, and go have some beer. If you're old enough, of course," I added. I slapped his back with a wet thwomp and he turned to stare at a group of teenagers in a bright rubber raft.

"What's the real estate, Dad?"

"The plot. In the cemetery. So when I go, you don't have a bit of trouble."

He didn't seem to hear me, or at least he didn't have any comment. We never did have much to say to each other. As my only son, I thought he'd at least appreciate it.

•

The cemetery mud covered my dress shoes like icing. I hate any shoe that attempts to put human toes into unnatural shapes and I drove home from Elysian Fields fast. Plus, my friend Cody was going to come pick me up before the social part of the funeral, which I knew from experience would last a long time and leave me in no condition to be behind the wheel. After our friend Roxy's funeral, I lost my license for a year and a half.

Cops don't take bereavement into account on DUIs.

Stepping out of my truck, I waved to my next door neighbor. Her long dark hair swirled around her head as she poured birdseed into one of her feeders. Every day she filled them up, and I had never seen so many birds around here. The word was out. When the neighbor lady wasn't watching birds, she shuttled her son back and forth to major cities, Washington, Baltimore, and Philly, to a bunch of doctors. The little kid was dying. That was probably what made her hands so nervous, always fluttering around. Still, she had a way of wearing blue jeans I could appreciate. But she couldn't be more than twenty-five and plus I could never remember her name. She had told me so many times that I couldn't ask again.

"You're all dressed up," she said.

"Yep. Funeral for one of my buddies."

Her face shut immediately. Are you not supposed to mention funerals to those with sick children? "I'm so sorry," she said in a voice that seemed more like a hum.

"Well, we're sad but not surprised. Little Roy lived hard," I replied. I tried to drag my shoes on the grass to scrape off some of the mud.

"Do you need anything?" she asked.

"No thanks. I'm just changing into something softer for the party. My friends throw a rowdy funeral."

She didn't even smile. I had said the word funeral again.

"I hope everything is a comfort," she said, stepping backwards onto her porch. I couldn't ever say the right thing. The next time I walked by her mailbox, I'd have to look closely, to see if it told me her name.

Birds pushed and argued as they swooped down to the newly filled feeder.

The summer rain had stopped but the land was saturated. Everything hung lower to the ground with the weight of water, and the air itself was heavy. Those birds sounded drunk with it. Right after rain, birds can hardly contain themselves. Changes in weather mean new plans, new flights, and new ideas.

In his sister's yard, Little Roy received the part of his send-off that he would have enjoyed; free beer, fresh barbeque, and his name as the center of conversation. Sure we all knew he overdosed, but we focused on the funny stuff. He once wrestled a live bear in a Charleston bar; we agreed that has to be illegal these days. We tried to name all his girlfriends, all his arrests, and all his lies.

Little Roy had the same legal name as his father, Big Roy. That fact allowed for many funny jokes and Little Roy's self-destruction. Big Roy had a prescription for Oxycontin, a big-time painkiller for small town folks, to ease his final days. That prescription put Little Roy in the ground. Usually, or at least in younger days, Little Roy could handle anything he put in his system, more than most men twice his size. Shots, tokes, enough acid that one time in Atlantic City to have him declared legally insane. Who would have thought that something from a doctor would have done him in?

"Little Roy would have loved this party," we said.

I had forgotten about the time he hid the frozen fish in his sister's car until she told the story. The guffaw caught me by surprise and I drooled salad dressing down my shirt. At least I wasn't wearing my one nice button-up anymore.

•

A.A. saved his marriage, but sobriety gave Cody a whole mess of us to drive home. After Cody dropped me off (with five drunk men still in the back of his pickup yet), I hesitated in the driveway, swaying slightly in what might have been a mild breeze.

Maybe I should knock on that pretty neighbor lady's door, whatever her name is. Show her what an older construction guy knows. Nailing. Screwing. Laying wood.

I made myself giggle and put a hand on my fence to steady the sway. Her window glowed.

Naw. If she started dating me she would gain weight. They all did. Something about me made women's sweet voices go shrill while their hips went wide. Then my friendly neighbor wouldn't be able to fit into those fine faded jeans. Plus, chances are she would say no to a scruffy man smelling like beer, salad dressing, and cigarettes. (All vices come back at funerals.) Besides, she had soft paperbacks split open all over her house. What kind of woman reads that many books at once? I felt pride at my logic. Patting myself on the back would have spun me off balance.

Still leaning on the fence, I felt the pack of Merits in my breast pocket. They weren't mine; I'd just grabbed them and the nearby matches from that table at Little Roy's sister's and started to smoke.

Little Roy would have been proud.

There was only one limp cigarette left. Pretty thorough for a non-smoker. The night stuck to my neck and cheeks; the humidity hadn't broken, just hankered down on the grass like dew.

After a few tries I managed to get my last smoke lit. Or whoever's last smoke. The fire jumped from the wooden match, suspended in the air for a moment, and then died. The gray air pushed into my throat and squatted in my lungs.

Something moved in the corner of my eye. Something yellow blurred above the fence.

A chicken? Maybe her birdfeeders actually attracted poultry, although my experience of chickens suggested that they weren't bright enough to fly around and scavenge. I blinked and focused.

Were chickens still able to fly? Or had domestication bred it out of them? I had seen a chicken hang-glide down off of a fence, but I had never really seen one fly. Did wild chickens fly? Was there any such thing as a wild chicken anymore?

With a graceful arc, the large chicken swooped away and then glided closer to the fence. The chicken wore yellow pajamas with white plastic feet. I closed my mouth around the cigarette, breathing the smoke out of my itching nostrils. Four feet in front of me, my neighbor's eight-year old son dove and leapt from the ground like a yellow leaf tossed by the wind.

I was proud of my calm silence; I made the transition from chicken to child without freaking out.

Maybe I am sick with fever, I thought. Maybe I am just way too drunk.

The boy jumped through the damp night air and paused before floating back down. He flung his thin arms in front of him to change direction. At the end of his yellow pajama arms, pale, fluttering hands had visible bruises. The chances that I was imagining all this onto some chicken in my neighbor's yard were slim. The spirals of motion began to make me feel the circles in my stomach. With a long arc, the boy veered towards the oak tree and seemed to toss a reproachful look in my direction.

Rocks skittered beneath my feet until I felt the concrete lip of my porch and stumbled up. I tried not to yelp as I bashed my shin, and tried not to fumble the door. Was this a miracle? Or a delusion? Or a scientific oddity? Anyone I called might think I was drunk and addled, seeing things on my way home from a funeral.

But even worse, people might run to ask that poor child questions.

•

Birds can fly because they are just barely enough stuff not to blow away when they scratch the earth for worms. Their bones are completely hollow, almost on the verge of collapse. You could snap a bird bone between two of your fingers. Instead of being a weakness, these eggshell bones are the reason that birds can move with the wind. Penguins have strong bones for climbing across icebergs and braving Arctic winds, but they lose the ability to fly. Other animals that can "fly" work on different principles. Bats and birds have hollow bones. Flying squirrels and flying fish—just stuck with the wrong name. Those things can't fly. They're just good jumpers. I looked everything up in my leatherette-bound, seven-volume *Encyclopedia Magnifica*, as I attempted to keep my hammering skull quiet. And I thought I would never use the things.

Thank goodness I could spend Saturday drinking cranberry juice and seltzer, leafing through encyclopedias. If I had to lift a hammer, I would be in serious trouble. Earlier in the week, the contractors had called to ask if I wanted double-time to finish the roof on the Sylvan Way job this weekend, but no one could say I lacked foresight. I turned them down flat. No way was a roof safe the day after a funeral. I was still in my robe when the mail came, and still in my robe when I walked the small hot length of my driveway to retrieve three catalogues and my electric bill. My head hurt.

"Hey, there," she said. I checked to make sure I wasn't hanging out of the robe. I must have looked like death.

"Hey," I said. "So what's wrong with Dell?" I had heard her calling to him, so I knew the boy's name at least. If only he called her something other than "Mom."

"Dew. Like Mountain Dew."

"Sorry. What's wrong with Dew?" I might as well know, since he was flying around my hallucinations.

"He's named after my uncle Dolittle. Except I couldn't quite give him the whole thing—just seemed too sad to stick a baby with such a depressing name."

"Dew is cute," I said. "Like springtime."

"Well, he has leukemia," she said, moving her hands around her shirt, as if she was wiping away dishwater. I felt a panic. My instincts for trouble sure hit home on this one. I had an urge for flight. I was no good to a woman with this kind of problem, my visions of birds were bullshit. She shoved her hands in her pockets to quiet them.

"Do you want a beer?" she asked.

I most certainly did, hair of the dog, but not here, not now. Not near her swept front porch by the twenty bird feeders. Not where I would have some responsibility to respond to what she just said. "Sure," I said.

I took a deep breath as the wood door banged crookedly behind her.

"I could tighten up those hinges for you," I offered.

"My boy is just being eaten, some kind of mutiny in his bones. Nothing I can do or say can help, because it's all on the inside, making him hollow," she said, running her hand violently through her hair. I felt evil for noticing the way her breast pushed upward with the motion of her hand. I turned away from her still-lovely stress, as Dew made a small sound on the couch. He did look hollow, an almost unnoticeable lump on a fine secondhand couch.

Water ran beneath the ground, birds covered my neighbor's trees squawking weather talk, and in between a boy in yellow pajamas defied gravity. Sick boys were supposed to be tied down with medicines and tubes, forbidden to jump and play. Now the ground could not keep him close, much less cover him up. All of it tumbled in my head like laundry, and I figured I must still be drunk from the night before. I needed to chug the light beer she handed me and to haul my ass back to bed.

•

Sunday, the official day of inertia, I wandered through my house picking up all the things I had knocked over or left out. Since my whole house reeked (a hot combo of stale beer, cigarettes, and old food) I threw open my windows and doors. My curvy neighbor stood sweeping her front porch.

"Hey, do you guys have a trampoline?" I asked. She put her hand on her hip and tilted her head like I was out of focus.

"No. That's not really something we thought to get."

"Good, good. Those things, well, they aren't any good anyhow. Kids fly off and some get paralyzed. Or worse." Why did talking to this woman compel me to bring up death and other deadly conditions? "Nope, tramps are definitely not safe."

"I won't buy one then. Do you let your son jump on one?"

"Who, Danny? No I don't think he would ever want to. He's not the athletic type."

"Does he ever come to visit?" she asked. And this was where women's mouths set in those lines, when they find out that Danny doesn't come over much. Even though he prefers to stay at his mom's house. I don't even have cable here, and the guest room is more of a closet. But women just shake their heads as if I chose everything just so.

"Sometimes. Well, I have to go to the cemetery. To check out my grave. I think someone is buried there. At least it seemed like it at the funeral." No sense even trying to dig out of this one. I turned and hightailed it to my truck. In my rearview mirror, I saw her fade back into the house.

The graveyard at high noon had quite a few visitors. Before checking my plot, I checked in on Little Roy. Someone had left him a full can of Budweiser amid all the flowers—maybe the guys did it Friday night. I leaned in to pick up the hot can and thought I would swoon from the sick-sweet smell of the sun-fading bouquets. Bud in hand, I stepped right onto the spot where I though his belly must be and pulled the tab. Luckily it didn't explode, although Little Roy would have gotten even more of a laugh. I poured the beer carefully onto the earth, ignoring the stares of some uncomfortably dressed couple.

I got my bearings carefully before going on to D409. It was right next to this lady's ex-husband who had D408. Or right next to where her ex-husband will be eventually. When they divorced, she had me come in and finish the basement. The guy had been promising to do it for years. She didn't really have any cash, so she signed over her cemetery plot to me, since she couldn't stand to be anywhere near her ex.

On D409, my grave, a twisted piece of driftwood now sat on top of the turned-up earth. No. Actually, the piece of driftwood was carved. What looked like a random shape from a distance, now clearly was a crude carving of either a swan or penguin. Probably a swan. Penguins don't seem like they would have the same sentimental value. Beneath the curve of the neck/wing, a ground-bouquet of violets wilted. Someone had been here in the last two days, maybe in the last two hours.

How many Mafia hit-men would return to place violets on the grave? Or to carve driftwood? Maybe some old guy just didn't really understand the rules on how to bury his wife, thinking he was still in the old country. Maybe some kids just buried a dog, a well-loved Rover. I felt a pang, remembering how broke up my son Danny had been when our old dog Zeppelin died. I forgot to tell him for a while; the dog stayed with me since the ex couldn't have pets in the condo they rented across town. I had already buried Zep when I told Danny on the phone. I could tell by the change in his breathing he had started to cry. The kid was probably old enough to take it better, but Zeppelin was the sweetest dog, even half-blind.

"Why didn't you tell me?" Danny said.

"I just did. Listen, I'm sorry. But he was old, a geezer in dog years."

"Did you bury him already?"

"Yep. Out by the clothesline."

At this Danny began to sob like a five-year-old, full of mucus and air. "I didn't even get to say goodbye," he said.

"For God's sake, Danny. He was dead. What's there to say goodbye to?"

I couldn't tell what was going on but the phone line rustled and crackled. Danny's mother finally came on the phone and said, "Can't you just be nice at all? Ever?" Now that I had just had a few words with Little Roy down at the cemetery, I felt bad about Danny not getting to talk to Zeppelin.

After work on Monday, I drove down to the Elysian Fields Cemetery office. After eyeing me (and my overalls) suspiciously, the Elysian Fields manager had promised to check into my grave break-in; he would "double-check the files" and let me know what happened. The cemetery man didn't look anything like what I imagined (corpse-y, creepy). Instead, he wore a button-down preppy shirt tucked into khaki pants. Some overgrown frat boy who managed gravesites instead of a bank.

I walked around while Mr. Preppie Grave did his detective thing. I was seeing more of Little Roy now than I had in the last three months of his final, pain-free binge. In those last days, he hadn't returned many calls. Cody and I thought he must have convinced another hot young thing with his crazy stories. After a few words with Little Roy (and righting the Bud can more firmly in the dirt in front of his stone so it wouldn't fall over every time it rained) I returned to my own real estate.

"Well, sir, do you have any relatives who knew about this plot?" the cemetery manager asked in a bill-collector's voice.

"What? No. Well, my son. Maybe my ex-wife?"

"Any chance that one of them would have used it without your permission?"

"Used my grave? It's not like borrowing the car."

"Sir, we have to ask. Not only do we have no records of anyone being interred in D409, your plot, but we have no records of any burials in that section since the Fourth."

"But that's two weeks ago. The ground there is freshly turned up."

"Yes, you're right. I checked it. Someone or something does seem to be buried. It could be some sort of a prank. Could you please check with your family members, and we'll proceed with the investigation on our side."

I wasn't about to call the ex.

Tuesday, we worked late. This lawyer wanted his fancy beach house finished so that he could throw a late-summer party for political friends. We went to high school with the guy. Back then he never had fun, never had a girl. We would pull away from school piled into Little Roy's orange Mustang laughing at people like him, with cave-fish skin and warped priorities. Driven folk never stayed around shore towns and we mostly never left. This guy's closets were going to be bigger than bedrooms.

When I got home, I stood in the rocky weeds of my yard. Should I call my ex-wife about the grave? No. Although she resented the hell out of me, she would have called if someone died. Across the fence, my fresh-faced neighbor sat varnishing a slab of wood, probably for another birdfeeder, singing Patsy Cline. I listened for a minute, lulled by her unsteady-but-sweet voice. Nearby, Dew reclined on a plastic lawn chair, with one pale arm flung above his head. Through half-closed eyes, he watched his mother's measured strokes in the darkening evening.

"Howdy, guys. Hi, Dew," I said, trying to make eye contact with him. "Aren't you up past bedtime?" She looked up at the sound of my voice and Patsy's song drifted off.

"I don't really have a bedtime," Dew said, lifting his thin arm off his eyes a bit. His head seemed too big for his fragile body, barely able to support its own weight, much less perform circus stunts. His eyebrows were falling out and he had that angel-child thing, the shine. I looked for a sign in his steady gaze and considered making some kind of a joke ("Hey kid, what's flying?"), but that would be a sure way to convince a mama I was a few eggs short of a dozen.

I wanted to ask Dew questions. How does it feel, Dew? Floating around at night? But his arm changed my mind. Inside his elbow sat tracks and lines worse than those of my friends dead of their demons. He was scarred up like any addict from poking and prodding, needles and tests. I could be someone who didn't ask dumb-ass questions about the kid's bones. And someone who didn't try to jump his mother's bones.

"Well, goodnight," I said. Both Dew and his mom mumbled.

After microwaving dinner, I pulled down the ladder to the attic, more of a crawlspace really, to find a few photos of Little Roy for some scrapbook Cody was making. I crawled over to the triangular window by the vent. I pushed and tugged but the thing seemed to be painted shut. I leaned against the glass (cool at least) and looked over the house next door. Her bedroom had a soft light, probably from a reading lamp next to her bed. I couldn't see anything except the corner of her dresser. A movement in the unlit backyard distracted me from feeling like dirty peeping Tom. I shaded my eyes from her bedroom glow, so they could adjust to the dim yard.

One still moment, and then yellow pajamas with white plastic feet kicked above the treeline.

•

At work on Wednesday, my head still felt like the attic, hot and too-full. A squirrel jumped over my feet on his way across the beams; I nearly tumbled off the roof.

"Man, I'm not going to your funeral next. Be careful," one of the boys below me said.

"I'm fine, like a cat."

"Yeah, you smell like it anyway." The boys cranked up the Eminem. My coworkers on the construction crew got younger and younger each year, many not old enough (or bright enough) to graduate from high school. Every other day I let them choose the music. Although they complained about Merle and Hank, I caught several of them singing along. Today, unfortunately, was their turn; the screech and discord barely distinguished itself from the sound of scrapes and hammers.

When I finally got home, I thought I conjured my neighbor's voice with just wishing. "Hey, could you come into my bathroom?" she called before I could get in my door.

"What is it you need?" I said, restraining myself from making the jokes that bubbled to my mouth, ever-present from years of bar-talk.

"I just—That came out wrong. My toilet won't stop running. I tried to pull up on that black plunger thing, but it just keeps going. It's been going for an hour or so and I really don't want to have to pay a plumber."

"Those fellows are crooked as pipes," I said. "Let me look at it."

"Thank you," she said. Her face had white spots on it, as if ice cubes had been held to different parts, but most likely she had just been crying a lot.

"Any news on the grave?" she said.

"Nope. No one knows anything. Not the cemetery manager, the coffin sellers, or the embalmer. There's only one embalmer in this po-dunk town, so he would know who's been done up or not."

She winced. I did it again, mentioning the town embalmer to someone might have to call him. Oh well. She brought it up. I rolled up my sleeve and tightened the water valve in her tank. Even with my hand up to the elbow in the pot, her bathroom smelled like Juicy Fruit gum.

I do miss how they smell.

By way of thanks, she insisted I stay for dinner. Just jar sauce and spaghetti with canned beans. But she cooked up the garlic bread spicy hot. Dew drove a Tonka earth-mover across the tablecloth.

"Sweetheart, eat your spaghetti," she said.

Lulled by tomatoes and candlelight, I almost answered.

"My belly still hurts," Dew answered. He smiled at her to deflect the concern that welled up in her eyes.

"Dew is being super-brave about chemotherapy," she said to no one in particular.

"Did you find out who they buried in your coffin?" Dew asked me. He must have been listening to us when we talked about D409.

"Not yet. The police are looking into it."

"Because they stole your plot?" she asked.

"No. I didn't even want to call them. But apparently burying a random body is a big-time crime. In case it's not just some hamster they have to proceed as if it's a big-time murder. So they need to do DNA and the works."

"What's DNA?" Dew asked.

"Stuff in your body that makes you different from anyone else," I said.

"Like leukemia?" asked Dew. His mother jumped up to refill his milk.

"Today I saw a blue jay, Dew, while you were napping," she said loudly. "It was so beautiful, the color of your Superman jammies."

After dinner I fetched my toolbox, to fix her back door. It didn't latch anymore. Doors and windows around here change shape in the heat and need to be pounded back into shape.

"Thank you for doing all of this," she said.

"Hey, no problem. You make better spaghetti than me."

"I used to be able to call the landlord for this kind of stuff. Owning a place is great and all. Dew needs the stability of it, but it's just that so much can go wrong."

"Murphy's Law."

"Do you own your place?"

"Nope. I rent."

She seemed to lean into the shoulder of my slightly damp t-shirt and breathe it in. With a last unnecessary tap, I put the Phillips head back in the box. The sky outside had faded, with the last light showing like a glow beneath a closed door. From somewhere behind her kitchen wall, pipes groaned.

"You can stay for a while, you know?" she said, allowing one of her fluttery hands to sit still on my forearm. "We could have a beer?"

Here it was. My invitation. I recognized the shininess in her eyes. I grabbed her hand for a minute.

I let her soft hand go and grabbed hard plastic of the toolbox handle.

The thing about real estate is you have to know when to get out.

Bunker

PHYSICAL EDUCATION

They had to dig. Sand crystals didn't stick to skin the same way that earth would. Sand collects in pockets, but it doesn't stain.

Even so, the small dark girl reminded herself to shower before coming back tonight. Some girls had no problem showering once, twice a day with fruity lathers but this one had to make a conscious effort. Struggling out of socks, jeans, shoes, t-shirts, and then having to choose new ones. The laborious attention to surfaces. Sand stuck to the parts of her skin letting moisture out.

"If we get used to it during daylight, we won't be scared when it's dark," her freckled friend had explained. The other freckled girl was the leader (taller, more boobalicious, better phone). The smaller girl (piano-playing, ethnic hodgepodge, better grades) liked handing over the decisions.

Her shoulder burned with the effort of moving sand, and the labored breath brought sand behind her teeth. The entrance wasn't easy to find; they circled the hill twice before the opening to the underground bunker appeared in the middle of a swell of sand.

AMERICAN HISTORY

"Why is this place so hard to find?" the smaller girl asked.

"They bulldozed sand over the entrance, so that nobody

could get in anymore."

"Because it's really dangerous?"

"Because they don't want anyone to know what went on down here. War crimes and stuff like that. During the war, they thought this might be one of the areas the Germans attacked. They were ready to be all secretive and take them out. But I mean, it's not dangerous. Tons of army guys worked down here every day," the leader said.

Only the very top of the door was visible, the metal teeth of its grate. They scrabbled up the sandhill and peered into the darkness. The air inside smelled cold, generated by something other than the ocean air outside. The girls dug into the sand, in front of four metal bars, one of which had been twisted to one side, creating an aperture large enough for a body to squeeze through. Head first down into the cave at an angle that made them push their hands ahead of them on the slope, waiting for the floor. "Shine the light down more," the leader said. They needed the light to touch the floor before palms did, before faces did.

The follower handed off the light. Her slimmer hips slid through the aperture easily and she dropped down onto the finally-flat surface.

The smell was earth, not the salty grit of sand. They were deep enough that the sand stopped and moist ground began. It was a great place to hide from the enemy. The smaller girl dug into the dirt until it pressed up against the softer half-circles of flesh beneath her fingernails. Then she dropped.

BIOLOGY

Earlier, by the tall faucet of a science classroom, a broad-shouldered boy swooped down on the taller girl and pressed his beaky nose into her clean hair. He inhaled and closed his eyes.

As the smaller girl watched, she wondered if no one gravitated toward her hair because she had not showered that day, or if the pull of the other girl went to the voice, to the boobs, to the far-wider smile. What part of popularity was breasts, and what part fastidious cleanliness? The taller girl put oils, lotions and fruity scents across everything bodily.

Although the tall girl walked with a certain sense of expectation, the science incident was startling to both of them. Later, the same popular boy grabbed the tall girl by the flesh on her upper arm. He half-dragged her to the shadows beneath the bleachers, kissed her so hard his teeth left purpling marks on her lower lip, and told her to meet him at a bunker later.

"You can bring a friend," he said.

LANGUAGE ARTS

Besides differences in the height of waves, the ocean never changed and neither local girl found the sight of it particularly interesting. Up the beach, the state park had more mystery, with its three tall observations towers positioned according to some antique war strategy. In the towers' shadows, subterranean bunkers lay officially dormant, part of a much deeper strategy and a darker surprise.

Arms entwined, the girls stepped down a long hallway in the central bunker. Each black door required a leap of faith to pass. The girls sliced the flashlight beam across darkness they hoped was empty.

"Aren't you glad we are doing this during the day, so that we know what to expect tonight?" the tall girl said into her friend's unshampooed hair.

"Why do they want to come here?" the small dark girl asked, skating the light across crumbling walls, bits of broken radios, cords reaching out to nothing. In one corner of the room, seven beer cans huddled, the skeletal remains of previous explorers. The smaller girl should have gone to band practice instead of following her friend. She should be sitting beneath florescent lights without her heartbeat dancing around her ears and eyebrows.

"Maybe this is what it's like to be buried," the tall girl said, turning away from the flashlight to stare back into the room they had just left. No matter how wide she opened them, her eyes could not adjust to blackness this total. She stumbled against a table corner, right on the still-sore spot where that confident boy had handled her. With a small sound, she sunk slowly from her heights, and sobbed. Her follower sunk beside her, put arms around the shaking shoulders and buried her nose in delicious hair. She squeezed her friend hard to keep the girl from sliding further down and puddling on the floor.

The small girl had to invent words, find ways to say what no one had ever said before, to say what no one understood.

"We're going to my house and we're not coming back," the small girl said. The other let herself be led.

MATHEMATICS

"They're not here." A tall boy scraped a flashlight beam across the sand.

"You think they chickened out?" the scrawny boy said to his broader friend, the leader.

"Yeah. Totally."

"So. It's just the two of us. You wanna go down there?"

"What's the point? We were gonna scare the girls. Let's go see if we can score a couple of beers from your brother."

Fire in the Hole

Daddy always wanted to be cremated. Being Catholic makes cremation impractical since, according to Father O'Malley, God only pays attention when you arrive in satin-lined oak with inlaid mother-of pearl. In the long, repetitive process of dying, Daddy told us again and again that he didn't want to be buried. But when the hour arose, Mama chose a shade of shell-pink for his satin pillow. Never in his life was Daddy a man to be ignored, and I can't help thinking that he had a hand in this fire.

Centralia burns now. His hometown. A rolling stretch of beauty, trees and ponds, peppered with sinkholes that snake down to the caverns below. Years ago, on the schoolbus, kids whispered stories of cows and children crippled or simply taken by the sinkholes. Today as I drove through the familiar passages and hollows, the place looked shell-shocked. Razed. Piles of rubble where houses stood and smoke rising, not from bombs but from cracks in the ground feeding oxygen to the subterranean coal fire. Centralia was a coal town. Now, instead of being chipped away by men choking on its dust, the coal burns in labyrinths beneath deserted streets and crumpled houses.

I return on a diplomatic mission. The impossibly skinny house where my stubborn aunties live has been bolstered by wooden supports on each side, to replace all of the demolished neighboring rowhouses. The three old women are going down with the ship, refusing the government's money and the safety of moving closer to Harrisburg.

Plenty of parking on the desolate street. Without the houses, I can see as far as the cemetery. Closer to the familiar blue door, the landscape makes sense to me again, if I ignore my peripheral vision. Here, sweet aunties would pat my head and give me a dollar when we packed the car to leave, every year without fail. Even last year.

"You have to be the voice of reason," my mother said. She fingered her necklace and hurried me on my mission. "Those old biddies are burning, and they act like they don't care. It's outlandish."

"Incidentally, it's also not safe. The town has been condemned," I said. The old women are not in danger of going up in a ball of flame as much as being pulled down by the ground collapsing beneath them as the fire slowly erodes ground support. Experts say this process could take up to fifteen years, but no other resident wanted to take a chance. My maiden aunts know full well they don't have fifteen years.

"Right. Of course it's not safe. And they were in that paper looking crazy." Embarrassment drove Mama's humanitarian project.

"What am I supposed to say if they don't want to leave? After all, they don't have much time left. Lots of people dying of cancer opt out of chemotherapy."

My mother crossed herself. "How can you even mention cancer?"

She did *not*, however, suggest that we exhume my father from the Centralia cemetery and move his final resting place somewhere cooler, even though his fine oak coffin would soon be *outlandishly* engulfed. Coal dust ate up his lungs, burning his breath until pieces of lung jumped out of his throat with each cough. She had disobeyed his final wish with the fancy casket and funeral hoopla—no one could accuse Mama of ignoring the significance of a burning bush.

Like the old women, he is staying put.

Right before I left home the blue plate dropped. Skip was late again and I could not keep my soapy fingers steady. That blue plate was part of my great-grandmother Mary Jean's wedding china, which she cocooned in her delicate undergarments to keep them safe in her trunk during the passage from Ireland. Clearly the shattered china was a sign.

My mother had warned me extensively about "shacking up," far more willing to have me marry a man she hated then to live with him in sin.

My common-law husband pulled up in a fire-engine-red truck that stood as high as our house. How small he looked jumping three feet down to the ground from its runner. I had just put my uniform in the dryer when the truck crashed up the driveway. Skip swaggered in calling for an argument. He swayed back and forth in rhythm with the thrusts of his accusatory finger. The fight heated up when I found out he took the money out of my savings account, all the insurance money. My three thousand dollar inheritance from my father.

"It's for you," he said. "A present."

"Great, Skip. Fantastic. How did you know that I wanted a monster truck?" Out the kitchen window, the thing burned red in the graying landscape of late fall. "Some present. And with my money. With my money. With my father's money." I started to cry, and the cat meowed, awakened from sleep by the electricity of my anger crackling through the house.

Skip mumbled something to the tune of "ungrateful bitch" and put on headphones to listen to old 80s metal way too loud. Trying to comfort the cat and myself with the same sobbing shush, I decided I had to go.

•

When the crooked blue door of the Centralia house swings inward, I can't see anything for a moment. The inside of the skinny structure is pitch dark in contrast to the clear November sun outside, hazed only slightly by smoke. Old Mare, née Mary, answers the door and welcomes me into the cool darkness.

"Who is it?" a sotto voice behind her asks.

"It's Denny and Laura's girl, all grown, come to visit us, Clara." I make a mental note that Clara is the blind one. I always forget. Clara and Jean are virtually indistinguishable, each with a speckled face and her own couch. I call them all "Auntie" to their faces and "Biddies" behind their backs, just like everyone does. Since one of her sisters lost both legs to diabetes and the other was partially paralyzed by a stroke three years ago, Old Mare's shuffling steps move for all of them. Old Mare still has her sight, though a helicopter left her with one glass eye. These women, folded like dumplings into faded couches, went to war with their brother—my father. When they returned from nursing overseas, they displayed the photos of their wartimes selves on the mantle and never left home again. We all assumed they had made some sort of pact, pledging their lives to each other and this rowhouse rather than to marriage, children, or careers.

The biddies offer cider and moist Oreos. Why did my mother think I could succeed where heavy-handed government officials failed? "Love speaks louder than the law," my mother said. But Mama's hope that I could help the family save face tempered her reaction when she saw my overloaded Chevy the day before.

"How long are you *staying*, honey?" she exclaimed. "You need to get up to Centralia as soon as possible. Is all of that laundry?"

"I left him," I said.

"Marriage is the promise we make that mends relationships," she said.

"Well, it didn't mend this one," I answered. "Isn't it wrong to marry someone you know for a fact you cannot love forever?"

"Here, hand me that coat before you drag it on the driveway. Why, when your Daddy and I first got married I wasn't even upset when him and his sisters went to war. I thought I would be glad for the time to myself. I didn't realize the true meaning of the marriage bond—"

She would have continued for hours, sing-songing how legitimization is love's glue, despite all the direct family evidence to the contrary.

"Mama, I'm too tired to talk and my heart hurts. I can't go back and really I don't need advice." Some drawstring tightened my mother's face. She opened her puckered mouth slowly but I jumped in before anything could get out.

"I need a good night's rest before I leave for Centralia."

That shut her up.

I'm already once divorced because because my mother wanted to save face at Saint Mary's. One sunny afternoon when I was home from college, my boyfriend and I made private space for ourselves in the back of my little green car. Somehow in the midst of coupling, an errant knee knocked the Chevy into gear and we crashed into the side of the empty house, which turned out to be a DC politician's ancestral home. Police wrote the "indecent behavior" part on the incident report. And even though she called him my "derelict communist boyfriend," Mama started planning which lunchmeat to serve at the wedding.

On our wedding night my new husband overindulged and called my relatives "capitalist pigs" and "bourgeois shits," forgetting that everyone wore blue collars here and he was the WASP. He couldn't walk, much less perform his husbandly duty.

•

Old Mare stares into a glass of gin at kitchen table. Her good eye winks when she smiles at me. She left the other one stuck to a helicopter blade in during the second World War; her lovely brown glass eye was prettier than her real one.

"Eh! What a little peach." My Auntie reaches her arms in my direction and smiles wider. She never says my name—I have too many cousins.

"Auntie, my mother wants me to talk to you about the fire." I sidestep her unsteady hands. I'm not sure if she is about to pinch my face.

"Give me a hug!" Old Mare says. "I got my eye on you, girlie girl! Eh!" Gin sloshes over the top of the glass she holds out as an offering.

I grab the glass before she dumps gin on the carpet and finds herself crawling around trying to find her prosthetic peeper. "God bless you," she murmurs.

"Yeah, well, God bless you too." I take a swig from the glass.

"Fire in the hole." My Auntie's real eye shines with approval as her wide brown prosthesis rolls at the bottom of the glass. This is her drunk party trick, usually reserved for the sanctified occasions: baptisms, weddings, funerals.

I kiss the crumpled left side of her face, all wrinkles and depressions without the support of the prosthesis. "There, are you happy now? Put your eye back before you lose it." I offer the glass.

She makes no move for her eye.

I figure the gin is sterile enough—alcohol and all—so I pluck Old Mare's eye from the drink. With my other hand, I lift up the folds of flesh. She sits like a dog letting a child turn its ears inside out. When the eye nestles in its hollow, it more or less looks at me.

"A bad marriage started the fire," she says.

I haven't told her anything about the fight, the truck, my suitcases.

"1940," she says. My auntie's story pins the fire on an unhappy Centralia housewife and a sinkhole behind a shed. This woman was preoccupied with her husband's erratic comings and goings, since he was a laid-off miner with a serious thirst. One night when he was late coming home, she threw his dinner, his grandfather's pocket watch, and the still burning logs from the parlor fire into the sinkhole.

Old Mare raises her thin eyebrows to indicate this angry moment in 1940 set the place ablaze.

I remember reading government officials think that a laid-off miner may have shoved a cigarette into a coal deposit to begin the slow burn. Either way, an old unhappiness on slow burn destroyed Centralia. I take another sip of her gin waiting for the right moment to speak my mother's words. All three of them talk, mapping out Centralia as it used to be, drawing its shapes and movements with stories, names, and a few inappropriate gestures. They have no comment about the world beyond this hometown, not since they came back from the war. I owned one of the photos of my aunties, back in the war days. In front of some species of plane, they stood arm in arm wearing bright nursing uniforms. I never have been able to tell which one is which. They all looked exactly like Amelia Earhart to me.

Finally, I lick Oreo from my fingers and get down to business. "Mary, Clara, Jean," I begin, with a serious breath. My aunties turn, lassoed by the conviction in my voice and the unfamiliar sound of their Christian names. I have to bring the conversation to the heart of the issue.

"Don't leave this house no matter what anyone says. Stick it out." The three women nod together, staring from serious wet eyes. "Don't sign any papers. If you love this place then you've gotta stick by it, even if it is burning." An auntie on a couch barks a little laugh.

"They can only force you to leave if the government declares it a national emergency, and those official folks are really slow about that sort of thing." I kiss three foreheads, soft as rumpled Kleenexes, and give each woman a ten-dollar bill. One of them, the blind one, runs her hand down the side of my face, perhaps with love, perhaps to see if I am real.

The three smile and say, "goodbye, dearie" while Old Mare shut their blue door against the smoke.

My mother will not be happy with this outcome.

This Centralia fire could just be another of Daddy's exhibitions in the face of Mama's press for "good manners." His voice boomed against Mama's brand of decency. The man from the insurance company told Daddy he should sue the mine for scorching his lungs, for killing him. My father just shrugged and said that would be like suing a snake for biting.

He always twisted jokes from sorrows. When his lungs pained him most, he took to supplementing his prescription painkillers with bourbon, carrying on the family tradition. Before he would down the warm whiskey (ice hurt his teeth), he would say, "Fire in the hole!"

Then toss it back.

It was from his days detonating land mines in the war; later he and his brother Ray made it their drinking toast. When Daddy drank away his morning pain alone in those last days, he would lift his left eyebrow as he said it, fully aware of his black humor.

My father would have gotten a kick out of the purple sweatsuit Old Mare wore to his funeral, the one that nearly gave my mother a stroke. But he didn't want some black-draped sobby service and didn't want to throw a bad party. He even gave away all of his personal effects himself, quickly and whimsically, to avoid post-mortem squabble.

My own personal effects are all crammed in my car. Luckily alcohol made Skip sleep like the dead when I clumped and banged in and out of closets taking everything of value. After the old Chevy was packed to the gills with my clothes and the cat toys, I stood, cat carrier on hip, in the shadow of the red truck with tires as tall as my shoulder. Here was my inheritance.

After the bad marriage to the socialist, I swore to myself and all my closest girlfriends that my next man would not be a self-styled intellectual. "No more politicos," I said. "They are terrible in the sack. Not enough exercise." We laughed until potato chips spit from our mouths, but careful what you wish for.

No one would call sexy Skip an intellectual, that's for sure.

If Daddy could have gotten an eyeful of the truck, he would have given Skip a piece of his mind. On my way out I grabbed the keys. Then I carefully poured a half a bag of sugar into its gas tank. "Sweetness speaks for itself," as my mother said.

Momentarily blinded by the hazy sun outside of my aunties' house, I give my eyes a chance to fit themselves to the situation. Instead of returning to the car, I head toward the graveyard. Since my father died, I have only been back a few times. I feel closer lines of communication when I close my eyes and think about him from the comfort of home than in a scrubby, smoking cemetery. Set in a once-lovely valley just two blocks from the biddies, the Centralia graveyard has some of the most visible ground damage from the underground fire. Cracks, opened by the heat below, gape between tilted gravestones. A Halloween landscape. The south side has a yawning crevice that I definitely don't want to crawl too close to, so I stay near the north bunch of birch next to Daddy's grave. A fissure has opened not four feet from his final resting place and I decide this is my portal.

I worry about collapsing ground, so I crawl commando

style. If the ground started to go, I would have more of a chance to hang on. A fissure leakes a thin stream of smoke. Could coal fire suddenly erupt, like a volcano? But this fire holds steady at a slow burn: an eruption is damn unlikely. I dart my hand into the smoke, and discover that the gray wisps are not even that hot.

Deep breath. I roll partially onto my side to work the keys out of my pants pocket. An offering for Daddy, like families who give their dead relatives wine to help them have fun in the afterworld. My father loved driving.

"Don't worry, I'm fine, and so are the aunties." My eyes blur for a minute. The smoke. I snake my arm forward and dangle the keys over the edge of the hole.

"See these keys? They're all yours. Do what you want." A low mumble from the ground almost sounds like the beginning of a laugh in Daddy's barrel chest. Plunging my hand into the thickest column of smoke, I let the keys drop. I lay on the ground long after the plinks stop, imagining Skip's keys bouncing off shelf after shelf of orange coal until they land in my Daddy's hand, now burnt as black as his lungs.

Love Song:

a Reproduction

"Let's go, kids."

A yellow bus emptied in front of a building full of statues, reproductions from "famous European artists, kids, the really famous ones." A bus-full of students, from that part of town where no one liked to go and where no art was on display, wandered in and out of rooms full of strangely familiar shapes.

A seventeen-year old wound up stairs. His teeth ached and "dentist" was only a word he read in school. The throb of other students disappeared when he got to an alcove to the left of the stairway. He stared at the most deliciously painful thing, a gray-green slave in marble. Although a metal square said the slave was dying, this boy did not believe it, not for a minute.

A lot happens before death.

The stone torso pulsed in the snug almost-summer. A thing that continues past the point of death, he thought. He placed two fingers in a hollow behind the statue's spine and rested his cheek on the curve of stone stomach, in an arrested dance. No alarms went off, no one watched him, not like at the bodega.

On a picnic table outside, the young man brushed away the gnats and reached into his backpack to pull out a sheet of paper. He felt its thickness between his thumb and forefinger, soft as skin. The world was underwater.

A whole class of them, angry and without aspiration, newly submerged.

And maybe those factories near school still leaked, or maybe the bodega corn had that fungus on it that once made people go crazy about witches. But the world got wavy.

Another breathless boy separated from a pack. He slept in a room with too many of his sisters, in an apartment where the TV talked the most of anyone. He waited for another to file past. In front of him, a green-gray statue. Somehow, these figures had appeared to him before, he had known them all. When the hiss of voices became a whisper, he approached the statue and placed one fluttering hand. And then the other. Waiting for the sirens, the infrared motion detectors to betray him. Boys like him should never put dirty fingers on things lovely like this.

Silence.

The stone was warm beneath his fingers, and he gasped. Barely breathing, he butterflied hands across the curve of the statue's stomach. When the stairs thumped behind him, the boy pulled away and felt like he was stepping out from sunlight back into the dark apartment.

Outside in the shadow of the bus, a young man pulled a peach from his backpack. Beneath the lonely students, leaning out of bus windows. He held the curved tension of the furred fruit.

"Hey, can I?" The other boy looked only at the fruit in the first one's hand.

He bit past the part that felt like skin, his soft tooth sending sharpness towards the top of his skull. And then, the sweetness.

The

New

Guy

Sleeping caused problems. Sleep, like drunkenness or truth serum, allows things to surface that by all rights should be kept underneath. The body relaxes into the rhythms and rejuvenation for a night and the mind goes nutso. Although I was standing up, I felt somehow that I was still asleep and struggled to focus my eyes. I didn't remember what I was dreaming, but I remembered the color red (comforting inside-a-womb red, not the oily red of crime scenes) surfacing. My name floated rhythmically into the color. And again.

James. James. James.

A light flashed.

I woke up standing in the new guy's kitchen: small, tidy, bare surfaces. This new guy held onto my upper arm; he looked not at me but at the lit screen of his cellphone. My mouth chewed of its own accord, moving strange shapes in paths between the points of my teeth.

My new gentleman friend stood in front of me, hazy but holding a very distinct cell phone. Sleep made my body heavy and my thinking slow.

I was chewing for some reason.

"What are you doing?" I asked. Why would this guy be up and playing with his cellphone? It had to be the middle of the night. The apartment was dark except for the metallic glow. Behind the phone, this new guy's angular face had cartoonish hollows created by the low light and my tired eyes.

I liked them thin.

"Look," he said, turning the phone's glow away from the planes of his face, and showed me a picture on the phone's small screen.

I swallowed.

"Who are you calling?" I said.

"Do you know where you are?"

"What?"

"Where are you right now, James?" The new guy wore only boxers, showing his strong pecs and blush of shadow where he shaved his chest. Vanity!

"Talking to you…next to the refrigerator." I ran my hand down the stubbly regrowth beneath his collarbone. "Hey, you left the fridge open."

"Do you know how you got here?" he asked.

"To your apartment?"

"To my kitchen."

I laughed. "I would call it more of a kitchenette," I said. I shut the refrigerator door with my foot and noticed I could taste blood.

He proffered the phone, and I dropped my hand from his chest to take it. On the screen, was a photograph of a guy, not quite as thin as my new guy, eating what looked to be strips of meat.

"Who is that?" I responded, slowly, somehow negotiating a mouthful of food.

"It's you," the guy explained. "Just a minute ago."

Okay. I looked again. My hair looked pretty good for the middle of the night, the curl not too out of control, and at least I didn't have the dreaded double-chin. My eyes were open but hooded, as if I was swooning over the cold cowflesh I ate in this small glowing picture.

That I was still eating.

•

Before that kitchenette moment, I had no idea what this variable was, the one tasting like death. This vegetarian had been waking up with a very strange taste in his mouth, but only when I stayed over.

His apartment was a wonderful place to stay, not just for the physical delights of the man who lived there but because several factors made it safe:

It was very clean, free of dust and allergen.

My new guy had those ropey muscles, there to provide protection, in case of break-in.

No doors went directly into the apartment from outside (most common mode of entry for burglars) and the windows were too small to crawl through.

These factors allowed me to let myself sleep, even though his snoring (he told me some story about "sleep apnea," but snoring, nonetheless) and movement kept the stretches short, the quality of the rest was far superior to what I could get at home. But recently, sleeping in my new guy's secure apartment had been leaving me with something strange and awful in my mouth. Every morning I kept getting the taste. I thought at first that I just needed to switch toothpastes, or brush my teeth for a more sustained period of time.

A rotting.

Strange tastes were unusual because I took great care not to introduce random elements. I monitored my own image, controlling my hair and keeping fit with constant walking. Restricted diet and diligent dental hygiene. I ate fresh vegetables, polenta, fruits, nothing that would taste of this deadness. Because I knew that alcohol was a form of poison that often opened the body to other invaders, I kept my intake to a social minimum. And after eating or drinking, I scrubbed and scraped the impurities from my teeth with an almost violent thoroughness.

Still, these recent mornings. The decay of flesh, the taste of death.

When the new guy stirred beside me, I would jump up to brush my teeth. People say you can't smell your own bad breath, but I certainly could. If he pressed a kiss on me before I could rush to the sink, I concentrated on not breathing, so that I wouldn't let any of small spots of rot float into his mouth on my breath.

"What am I doing here?" I asked, unsure if I meant why I was standing in on the linoleum or what I ate in that glowing image.

"You're eating Thai beef and broccoli from SweetGrass. Mostly the beef. My meat has been disappearing lately—*ha, ha*—but really, and I didn't know where it went. You've been a carnivore at night."

"Why didn't you wake me up?" Beef. That was what was in my mouth.

"I thought you weren't supposed to wake up sleepwalkers."

"But it doesn't really look like I'm walking." Only my hand and jaw showed any movement in the glowing photo.

"Sleep-eaters then. You've been doing it a lot."

The taste in my mouth.

"Pretty much every time you've been over. You kept up and I was trying to figure out what the hell you were doing. Last week I made myself wake up and you were finishing my leftover hamburger."

"But I don't remember any of this. Why didn't you tell me?"

"I know how you are about evidence, James. I didn't think you'd believe me unless I had some kind of proof."

"So you just led me back to bed?"

"I let you finish the burger first."

While I was sleeping, my body acted of its own accord, against all of my conscious policies. The thought that I could be acting, or even worse talking, when I was not awake to run interference was awful. It would be like being very very drunk—I had watched so many people in bars reveal all their secrets and begin to cry. Even worse, their faces slacked into grotesque exaggerations.

I chose never to get very very drunk not because it didn't seem fun but because I couldn't stand the idea of letting my face and secrets go like that. Like being my mother.

The nighttime failure of my vegetarian lifestyle was just one of the ways that I betrayed my best intentions around the new guy, who I wanted to know only the most wonderful version of me. Something about this broad-shouldered, well-shaven man and his clean apartment made me just as bad as those melting-faced drunks. Only sober. Certainly, the body can be controlled, contained, tamped. But then if the mind's defenses slack, the body rises up and takes the driver's seat. Statistically, the top four times that humans lose mental control and give over to the bodily demands at odds with logic or the law are:

1—*sleep (the state of sleeping or the state of sleeplessness)*
2—*alcohol*
3—*drugs*
4—*desire (can be sexual or for basic nourishment)*

When any of these four factors are combined, the effects are intensified. Most people convicted of a major crime use at least one of these four as part of their defense strategy. Each time the new guy got close my rational self-talk failed (*I should smile, I should throw my shoulders back, I should not mention that*), then I no longer took instruction from my mind. My body outstripped my civilized intellect, sort of like what the moon does to werewolves. The most mild-mannered professor becomes nothing more than an animal when presented with just the right combination of external factors.

Something about the new guy made my body act in horrifying ways. My beautiful, blood-fed boy. I could feel his voice purr inside my own body when he put sound waves into the air. And even worse was what rose in my throat. I bit my tongue to strangle words because I couldn't trust myself not to spit them out.

I love you.

Desire has signals that the body cannot falsify. When two human animals have a mutual attraction, their pupils contract upon eye contact. Rapidly. My eyes dilated every time he walked into the room. His broad shoulders brushed against door frames and cars with the pure assertion of bulk. Sometimes he would move away from me, sometimes he would raise the left side of his lips in his lopsided grin and I would feel my mouth begin to form preposterous phrases.

I love you.

Sometimes, late at night, bodies revel in everything that they are denied for the rest of the day. All the rules and strictures of the confined and socially appropriate person fall to the wayside in light of everything that happens under the cover of darkness and the freedom of the semi/un-conscious. When women fall asleep and dream of being raped by their oppressors. When the last thought of the day is of the sheer relief that the worst-case scenario would offer.

"I can't believe I just did that," I said, wiping my mouth. The small image still glowed.

"Yep," he said, recapping. "I think it's been every time you've stayed here."

"But that's, like, a month. Even if you were scared to wake me up why didn't you *say* something in the morning?"

"I wasn't even sure it was you at first. I thought maybe I was doing it. I'm the one with all the sleep issues," he said. "You always waited until I was asleep to pop the fridge."

My anger rose because part of our connection was the understanding: my desire for control with careful regulation, the kind that makes people live forever and have great skin tone (he cared far more for living forever than skin tone.) He and I had different ideas about what to restrict. He avoided dairy, sugar and fats. For the new guy, protein reigned supreme—sinew was manly, white flour too soft. He ate a Keto-esque diet meant to build his muscle, and although we could always share fish and steamed veggies, the beef was his alone.

I thought about Mad Cow disease and gave a whimper.

"Maybe you deprive yourself so much that your body is rebelling," he said, walking back toward the futon and placing the icy blue vodka bottle on the bedside table. In his studio apartment only about eleven steps separated the refrigerator from the futon.

"I don't want to eat these things," I said, my voice uncomfortably high. How dare he judge? He seemed enamored with my trim figure and bright eyes.

"You seem to want them when you're sleeping."

This from a guy who was crawling into special sheets, designed so that microscopic bugs couldn't crawl on him in the night. Everyone who swears that they like the ways in which they abuse or deprive themselves sounds the same, I imagine. Every Patty Hearst who joined her captors rather than feel quite so alone. But I really *didn't* like the taste of meat, at least not when I thought about my arteries and the living animal, host to all kinds of parasites and bacteria. But here it was. The Thai beef still lingering on my tongue and the photo of my eyes half-closed with my mouth open in a masticating ecstasy.

It couldn't be me. I didn't *eat* meat.

I put down the cell phone and sat beside him on his expensive, mite-repelling bedclothes. I grabbed his hard shoulder. "Now I could get Mad Cow disease."

"James, they've totally contained Mad Cow disease," the new guy assured me. I noticed his hair thinned on the very top.

"It turns cow brains into sponges and it'll do the same to humans," I said.

"Only a couple of English milkmaids actually died, I swear." How could he be so casual?

The new guy laughed as if I had accidentally farted (a small bodily betrayal), rather than done awful things while sleeping (a huge bodily betrayal).

"Cheer up, James. I'll tell you a joke," he said, snuggling back down beneath those sheets as I sat over him. "This one cow turns to another cow and asks, 'Hey are you worried about getting Mad Cow Disease?'" He patted the tartan comforter, suggesting that I lie beside him. I remained sitting. "And the other cow says, 'Why would I be worried? I'm not a cow, I'm a helicopter.'" He giggled, a sound more like a gargle. As I waited for him to notice that I wasn't amused, that I was scarred and scared, his breathing became more dramatic and he slid into slumber.

Laughing, sleeping. My need for comfort turned to anger. I wanted to slap him back awake. But his unagitated face, softer in sleep, was unslappable.

For a moment, I lay down beside him, without getting beneath the covers. I listened to his raspy breathing, and maybe half-slept in the spaces between exhales, but the image came back: I was standing (again!) in the cold air and wan light of his refrigerator, holding a slick Styrofoam suitcase full of leftovers. I never wanted to sleep again, at least not in an apartment stocked with beef for my subconscious hunger. Plus, how could he think this was some kind of *joke*?

Without waking him up, I pulled on my shoes and jacket.

I had to get out of his apartment. Sleep, for me, had become something much more frightening, a place where I became some other guy.

Scrap

"Anyone can cook with a recipe. How hard is it to paint by numbers?" Our mother flung open cabinets and pulled out dusty cans, the ones way in the back.

Tonight she cooked.

We stayed within earshot but scooted out of the way.

When the check didn't come in time, we stayed away from the bright grocery store. We hadn't been there in three weeks. The cupboards were fairly bare. Two nights in a row we mixed up envelopes of instant oatmeal, while our mother stayed locked in her room. Earlier that evening she had smoked at the table, crunching a pulled-up linoleum strip with her toe for nearly an hour. We all were startled when she jumped up and turned on the radio.

"Giddee up, a oom-bop, a oom-bop, a maow-maow," she sang and began to dig. The kitchen yielded white soup, canned pumpkin for pie, a bottomful of tube noodles, ketchup, pillowy lima beans, and a hardened scrap of Swiss.

When Red got home, nearly directly after his job, he found a nearly complete casserole steaming up the kitchen windows.

"Smells great in here." He had to bend to get through the door, and brought with him the sting-smell of gasoline and cigarettes.

"Just making soup from stones, baby." But she was laughing. At these moments the whole world loved her, no matter what hard parts you could see around her mouth. And when we balanced our plates on our knees (the table could only hold three of us at time) she accepted our praise as her due.

"Kids, you know that's my talent," she said, blowing on a steaming forkful of casserole. "Anyone can make dinner with heaps of ingredients—that takes nothing special. Anyone can wind up a player piano, too."

Once we were all watching cable and a bunch of men in tight coats rode their horses after a whole pack of dogs. All the hoopla was for one ratty little fox. The thing amazed us—all those fancy clothes and barking dogs to see if they could catch a single animal. We laughed and pointed but our mother woke out of a half-sleep to rail at the world.

"Turn it off!" she yelled. She fumbled with the remote. Eventually she turned the channel to some cop show. "Some people can't do a goddam thing for themselves," she said, and lit a cigarette with a shaking hand. We all nodded our agreement, and watched the new channel. She had the same reaction to cooking shows where people in bathrobes and tall hats mixed exotic ingredients in shiny places that looked more like hospitals than kitchens.

"This is pretty damn good," Red said, reaching for another ladle-full.

"Mom, this is really yummy," we chimed in.

We all agreed it was like magic, and mostly forgot that there had been any cans of soup left. We wanted her to pull dinner from her palms, like a magician's scarf, and mostly she did.

Tuesday, Red had the sideways in his walk, the smell of whiskey mixed with the gas. "Where's your mother?"

We weren't sure. The bus had dropped us off hours before and we had made lots of noise to fill the house, but not the right kind, not the satisfying rumble beneath her voice. Each day, we would chat as we walked up the road. But as we got closer to the blue house we quieted, listening for her. Spring days when she hung clothes on the line, or fall afternoons where we found twenty people there before us squirting lighter fluid into the barbecue pit, or dark winter days where the hum of the heater and the tightly sealed windows kept us in the dark until the door squeaked open and suddenly Merle Haggard's singing swelled out—those moments were like finding the secret passageway open. She only put on the music when she was happy.

Tuesday, however, she was gone. When Red's truck lumbered up the road, we all hummed with excitement while not jinxing anything by jumping up or commenting. Maybe they had gone together somewhere and she would jump out of the cab, happy and smelling of smoke.

Even if she was drunk and a little mean, a random slap was better than her absence. Better if she looked at us and made sharp comments about our schoolwork, our expression, or our daddy, than if she sat and wouldn't see us. And then locked herself in her room, with or without Red.

We didn't mind Red, who now seemed to live with us. He brought us together, giving us a new focus as we crowded around his saggy form on the couch.

"Girls, your mother don't love me anymore."

His weak voice and unfocused eyes horrified us. His watery eyes were even more horrifying. Because, of course, we all wondered if and when she would stop loving each of us. Nothing was guaranteed.

But how dare he say it?

"Last night, she was a wildcat," he said drinking a long swig of his Budweiser, pressing his tongue against the silver can. Cats sometimes screamed up on Bald Knob, and sometimes laughter with other noises floated from beneath their bedroom door. But proximities to wildlife and the bedroom goings-on were still mysterious. What exactly was wrong with our mother's wildness? She certainly she didn't hide the sharp parts of herself very much, mostly just from people who came to the restaurant or the people in charge of stuff.

"There's dinner..." we started to say. The baked bean smell didn't distract him.

"But it wasn't me. She was wild, but she wasn't there, you know what I mean."

We didn't know what Red meant.

Except for her daydreamy stuff, where she would stare and smoke and look right through us. Last night, when she cooked, she didn't drink, because there wasn't anything in the house. So we couldn't think of what would be so differently wild. "She got more outta it than I put into it," he said.

Now we were really lost. Red's eyes leaked tears and his breath huffed. We wanted to hurt him (pinch him, kick him, punch him) for both telling us more than we could get, and because maybe he drove her away. "It had to be somebody else, it sure wasn't me," he said. "She's gotta be thinking on someone else."

The metallic scrape pulled us all around. Her hip pushed the door open.

"What's wrong with all of you?" she asked. Red lifted his blotchy face from the curved corner of the couch. Mom flicked her eyes away from his face immediately and sighed. "Are you cooking something?"

We nodded, but couldn't quite move yet. Red made a small sound.

She refused to dignify Red's squeak. It might have said "baby." Instead, she squeezed past all of us, pushed our various papers to the side, and set down the grocery bags on the kitchen table. The check must have come through, or she sweet-talked the cashiers again. Or something. She could make a snake lend her its skin for a few weeks. The baked beans hissed and spit a bit over the side of the pan.

"What have we here?" She slid the spatula around the pot's curve. She turned down the burner, and leaned against the counter.

"I can't do it," Red said, hunched over himself by the table.

"Honey," she said to any of us, "get me that chicken out of the bag."

The

Consistency

of Dubbie

My mom calls it "shaping." As in, we really shaped that shopkeeper/motel clerk/principal. Most of the time we do it to save money, get a place to stay, or keep from getting in trouble. Her name changes every time, but I am always Dubbie.

I can fold up my limbs, and speak very simply. Then I am four years younger and get the "Seven and Under Eat Free" deal at the Beef Barn. My mom says we are running from spies. We are running, at least.

"How dreary to live like everyone else, what a rut," she says. Everyone tells me she is beautiful.

True stories: We really did live in a bus, tell fortunes on a boardwalk, and drive our car off an icy cliff to cradle safely in a tree. What scares me are the stories that are in between, true stuff shaped past recognition. Sometimes I forget which things really happened. I don't know what Dubbie stands for. Once when we were Russian refuges she said it was short for Dubroyevski. Another time, picking crabs in a country club, she told the waiter that I was Dubwell Dupont IV, of carpet and paint fame. When she explains my name, I get caught in a bit of trance. One could be true.

He knows my name.

"Dubbie, I found you."

No movement in his voice, just a flat road. His eyes don't

move, barely blinking. Mostly his hands stay quiet in his lap. Only a few curls on his head move, curls like mine.

He carefully writes his name and address in capital letters across his rent-a-car agreement. With a careful sigh, the probably-dad-man folds up the yellow paper and hands it to me.

The name on the piece of paper: Dubran Stanfield II.

"I'm about to leave for cello camp, but I'll give you a call from there," I say.

We make shapes and the world has to be the cutout around us.

"I really shaped him," I tell my mother with the birdlike hands.

"That's my boy, Dubbie," she says and pulls the suitcase from beneath the bed.

The
Upward
Spiral

Buzzing meadows make your head hurt and your bladder squirm. In summertime, the road unfurls in unbearable, shimmering lines, while you hardly have enough moisture to sweat, despite the heat.

Driving across the empty states, you always feel the press. You have to pee. Again.

You could wait for a green sign, for those rows of colorful preservatives and refrigerated bottles. No.

You yank the car to the side of the shimmering road, which may not be the right road at all. You step over what looks to be a broken wagon yoke. Someone put that here as a joke, maybe. No one uses wagons. Insects blur around you. You head between two earthen buildings collapsing into themselves. Sounds of electricity whir, but you know this time, it is all wings.

Fly-over country. Full of nonsense like wagon parts. Electric with insects. You never see the once-cellar that you step into, and you don't remember the fall.

Cellar door—the most beautiful phrase in the English language.

Whether or not you pee on the way down, you can't be sure.

"Bears, skunks and badgers," the young beekeeper says. You can tell he's a beekeeper because he has a hat like a Victorian bride, full of net, but ready for adventure.

"Congratulations," you say.

The boy leans over. "Though we are far enough from the hills that we rarely see bears. And of course the wax moth. Sometimes I sit next to the hives for hours, real still, and wait for wax moths."

This young man, of the impossibly long eyelashes, spoons golden ooze onto your wounds. "Sir, I promise the honey will help," he says and continues to emphasize the importance of protecting his hives. You want to mention the "sir" but your mouth won't shape the words. "When I can't stay up all night, or if there is a whole posse of moths, I light the lantern. And put a whole bucket of water right beneath the lamp, full of lye soap. The moths must be torn between the honeycomb and the flame, but they can't ignore the lantern or their own reflections."

The next morning, the brown-eyed boy wraps your head injury in a loosely woven white cloth. On your left side, the cloth drapes over your eye. With right eye closed, you see the world through white grids, a series of miniatures. The boy details bees disemboweling themselves post-sting. No wonder they've abandoned everything.

The dizziness flutters your eyelashes.

"Those people think that beekeepers never get stung. Of course they do," the boy continues and proffers his arms. Long, golden, flecked with small scars. You let your eyelids fall and touch the slightly raised surfaces.

"Doesn't it hurt?" you ask, wanting to read meaning into the marks his fingertips skated between.

"No. It keeps me in touch."

The buzzing in the air moves to skin and that very back part of your tongue. After four days, the boy mentions the phone, and you call for a ride. You must find words to describe where you are. As he stands beside you on the porch, looking into the fading light, the sound swells.

A sharp point.

You don't see the doomed bee, the one who ventured beneath. You feel the sharp sting and imagine the resulting struggle. A warm circle spreads from the point on the flesh of your left calf. Closing your eyes, you sway slightly. Has it disengaged, begun its descent? This is where they go, the wagon wheels and open cellar doors, beautifully phrased in the darkening prairie.

You grab fistfuls of the boy's soft soft shirt to keep upright. Wax moths flicker towards the porchlight.

A dead bee falls, and a motor hums just over the horizon.

Luck
Be a
Lady

Although we gasped and shook our heads when Jebediah Turner ended up in jail for stealing his wife's severed foot, we all wondered if we would do the same thing. Or more to the point: if anyone would love us enough to steal back our body parts from County General.

When his wife, Edith, testified that the foot was hers, though the hospital called it "medical waste," their lawyer argued that no one could be prosecuted for stealing something that legally belonged to his wife. We all knew that Mr. Thaddeus J. Ebbers, Esq. hadn't made very compelling arguments since his wife left him for a high school senior, but we complimented his silver tongue after Jebediah's acquittal. More compelling than Thaddeus's grandstanding might have been Jebediah's arm down around Edith's waist as she hobbled into the courthouse.

In his youth, Jebediah Turner had broken both legs jumping off of a barn, joined the Navy for fourteen days, and sworn never to return to his hometown. We all hoped he would return, ready to marry any of us and to bring his fiery laughter back. No other black-haired boy before or after Jebediah had lit us up in quite the same way. But when he did return, by his side was a woman our age with the hair of a teenager, long, brown, and unrestrained. A bit like Cher in sensible clothes.

Her name was Edith. We never did find out her last name,

since Jebediah kept calling her Mrs. Turner. Later, Massie Rozinsky let it slip down at the post office that "Mrs. Turner" wasn't yet divorced from the man she left for Jebediah. Not that Jeb seemed to give a damn. He wound his arm around Edith and would occasionally rest his chin on the top of her shiny brown hair. At least he hadn't come back with one of those tall blond Amazon women. That would have been worse. The ankle we could handle.

He brought this small woman he called "wife" back to meet his parents, but ended up purchasing property. When Edith's foot started throbbing they turned the truck onto a dirt road and climbed through pine trees to the overlook above a porous bowl of lush land choked with viney vegetation and pocked with rumbling holes from underground streams. Jebediah stared in wonder while Edith's foot threatened to jump out of her shoe. "We'll find our fortunes here," she said, wrapping her arms tighter around Jebediah's waist. They bought the land the next morning (Ronnie Rexrode had been trying to sell it off for seven years) with the lottery money that resulted from Edith's itch in a Kentucky 7-11, and posted a plywood sign on the Ponderosa pine: "Turner's Point." Edith painted the sign with red toenail polish from her purse. They were home.

The first person Edith opened up to was Massie Rozinsky, who drove up to Turner's Point every day to deliver mail. Those of us on Massie's route knew she never kept a strict schedule or cared about the calories in proffered cups of hot chocolate, and Edith always had questions about the mail. Over several weeks, Massie dropped bits of information as she wound through the valley.

Ever since she was just a girl, Edith had a gift. When she was five years old, her mother could not find the wedding ring that she had flung away from her in a fury. After searching the entire house, the frayed woman threw herself across the couch and sobbed.

"Edie, Edie, what have I done?! I lost it. What I am going to do, Baby?" Edith's mother cried. (When Massie Rozinky told the story she did the mother's voice in a drunken Elizabeth Taylor kind of way.) Edith, her young, tangled-headed daughter stood by her side for almost an hour before the woman paid attention.

"Mommy, my foot thinks the ring is in the disposal." Without questioning her daughter's sources, the red-faced woman thrust her hand into the potato and carrot scraps and came up with her cubic zirconia set in real gold. She squealed and hugged her daughter; she even bent down and showered kisses on Edith's small blue flip-flopped foot.

"You listen to your body, Baby. It knows. It knows." Her young mother wiped a bit of sludge off of her ring, screwed it on, and splayed her fingers in front of them. They both smiled. Lifting the ringed hand, Edith's mother swept her thumb down her daughter's cheekbone. "Yes, Edie, it knows," she repeated. Ever since that day, Edith jumped foot first into her future. We all knew about Jebediah and the lottery, so the minute anyone saw Edith buying up something, even if it was just beef jerky, no one could help but buy some too. Just in case.

We came under the cover of casseroles, searching for secrets of their coupledom as we glanced inside their cabin, and invited Jebediah and Edith to various events. They started to accept. At baby showers and barbecues, Edith filled us in. We listened intently, but sometimes just to gather bits of evidence. The only thing that threw Edith off track was her first husband. For fifteen years Edith's foot went numb as she puttered around a clapboard house, playing wife to a Tom Jenkins from Ohio—a distant cousin to the Cass Jenkinses. He ended up turning to taxidermy (partially in their kitchen) and other women.

"Didn't your ankle tell you not to marry that man?" we asked. "How could it lead you to Jebediah and not warn you about the wrong one?"

"I thought the fact that my ankle was silent was my answer," Edith replied in her slightly raspy voice (we imagined she had spent her dissolute youth smoking several packs a day even though she must have quit.)

When they necked on the porch, behind Tom's barn and in his car, Edith felt the same kind of itch she felt in her ankle, except in other places. "I thought that was the message," she told us. "Maybe the feeling I was supposed to get when I knew. After that I never felt a thing in my foot. I thought maybe because I had reached my destination." Even though, apparently, from what Edith intimated in other conversations, those other currents barely rippled once the hot flush of adolescence faded.

Edith didn't love talking about Tom Jenkins, but we could always press her at Christmas parties to tell us about meeting Jebediah Turner in that parking lot. We would drag up someone who hadn't heard the story before, an excuse to get her to tell it again.

"I couldn't find my car," she always began. "A blue Ford." We all pictured a mall, a real one with more than just a Sears. In this real-mall parking lot, Edith walked in circles and could not remember for the life of her where she parked that car. Edith decided to close her eyes and spin around slowly, hoping to end up pointing in the right direction (this was where Edith's impracticality lived up to her younger-girl hair and flowing skirts). Spinning slowly as she counted, Edith planned to count to seven, her favorite number: the needles in her foot made her stop at two. Like something asleep coming back to life, Edith's lucky foot buzzed with a lunatic rhythm. She hadn't felt anything more meaningful than an ingrown toenail in more than ten years.

And there he was.

When Edith opened her eyes, Jebediah Turner stood transfixed in front of her. We could all picture this moment, his green eyes and Cherokee color from his mother's side. That tilt of his head that pokes his squarish jaw forward. The black tufts of hair swirling away from his cowlick. Neither one really remembered what kind of small talk they made (although we pressed them for their first words), but Edith left the blue Ford in the parking lot and never looked back. She wrote a polite letter to Tom, telling him the general location of the car and asking would he please sign the divorce papers. According to Massie Rozinsky, who must have thanked her lucky stars for her new mail route, Edith asked everyday about official documents arriving from Ohio.

That jump out of the barn had busted Jebediah's left eardrum, which eventually gave him an excuse to leave the Navy. He told Edith that he had been hearing a ringing in his ears for close to year now, like the whine of a drill four doors down. Earlier, he told his parents that the ringing was caused by them specifically (right before he hightailed it to the Navy). All we knew was just that he always was listening to something else, trying to shrug it off when we vied for his attention. That day in the parking lot the whine had gotten louder as he walked closer to the small woman turning with her shopping bags spinning out. When Edith opened her eyes, Jebediah's ears stopped ringing abruptly.

"That 'hello' was the cleanest sound in the world," Jebediah said to a bunch of us during Pioneer Days. We sighed and smiled.

Edith's foot did not go dead again. Anytime she was near Jebediah her toes prickled; we often stared at her shoes and longed for sandal weather, so we could see what changes Jeb wrought in that foot. The portentous whole-foot pin and needle ache would hit at key moments, like at the 7-11. As Jebediah waited in line to pay for the gas at a stop along the way, Edith grabbed sodas from the cooler. When she stepped next to her husband in line, her foot made so much ruckus that it threw her off balance. She thought at first that her right foot and ankle revisited the throes of her new love, but then she realized that Jebediah's left hand rested on the lottery machine. "We have to buy a lottery ticket Jebediah," Edith said. Her husband ordered ten and when the next day's numbers were posted they were one hundred thousand dollars richer, minus tax.

Three days later, Edith turned her ankle in a sinkhole set in the fertile porous valley beneath Turner's Point. As she left Jebediah that morning, she called, "Don't expect me to come walking back until I find more fortunes!" They both laughed and exchanged one more kiss. Edith was letting the palpitation in her foot and ankle lead in exploring the thirty-seven acres. Her ankle turned as her foot slid into the underground stream and her head hit a sharp outgrowth of rock on the way down. She realized that she had been with Jebediah for thirty-seven perfect days and smiled at her good fortune before her whole body was eclipsed by the pin and needle sensation emanating from both her ankle and the wound on her brow.

Busy putting a porch on their cabin, Jebediah didn't even worry about his wife until nightfall. When Massie Rozinsky walked their catalogues inside and asked after Edith, Jebediah shrugged. He figured she followed her foot to the far reaches of the thirty-seven acres, looking in every tree hollow for the riches her body promised. When the day thickened into night, Jebediah began to worry and paced the thirty-seven acres.

Not until the daylight did Jebediah locate her small

form pressed close to the ground. When he saw her pale and crumpled, foot twisted in a sinkhole, he cursed his faith. Jebediah struggled with her body up the hill home, and drove to County General with her head in his lap, her lucky ankle poking out the truck window into the thick summertime air. A few of us drove past and thought the show of affection while driving a bit ostentatious, not knowing.

In court, Jebediah told everyone that a high-pitched drone like a swarm of bees filled his ears. With tears in his eyes, he told everyone that he thought she was already dead. Why should he lift her body into someone else's arms? For someone else to sanitize and scrutinize? His Edith would not to be delivered thus. No, even against the newfangled laws that wanted to keep you in order even after death, Jebediah would bury his wife himself. We all felt our eyes filling up as he described the plan of his despair. He would get the shovel and find a beautiful spot so she could rest above the tips of the trees, sharp pine points made soft by the distance, trembling and shaking with the wind, making the whole valley shimmer like a body of water.

Perhaps as a reward to his virtuous decision, Edith opened her eyes. "Baby, my head hurts," she said. Jebediah skidded over to the side of the road and cradled his wife in a cloud of dust.

"It's your leg I'm worried about, Edie. You lost lots of blood."

"My leg doesn't hurt. I can't feel a thing."

Once they got to the hospital, we all knew what happened. The testimony at this point could have been spoken by any one of us sitting in that courtroom: she lost the foot, ankle included.

When the straight-backed Frances Rampling, R.N, with an angry line cutting across her broad forehead, approached Jebediah's plastic chair, he knew the news had to be bad.

"I'm sorry, Mr. Turner, but we couldn't save her leg," Frances said shaking her head briskly. Several of us found ourselves shaking our heads in tempo with the story. Frances played herself on the stand and shook her head more vigorously so as to show off her new perm.

"But my wife—she's okay?" When Jebediah repeated his words in court, the judge stopped to mention that Edith Jenkins was not legally his wife. Jebediah pretended not to hear.

"She should be fine," Frances replied in her clipped "I'm a medical professional" tone. "We had to amputate below the left knee. She's weak from the blood loss and may experience shadow pains." Frances continued to catalogue the medical specifics but all Jebediah could do was smile.

"Mr. Turner? Sir?"

Frances's sharp voice penetrated his happy silent haze. She asked again if he would like to see Edith, who would be waking from the anesthesia any moment.

"Yes, yes, of course. But I have a question." Jebediah shook his legs out of the small chair and tilted his head. Frances recalls the head tilt very clearly. When he stood up he realized that he stood a full foot taller than the severe nurse who had been the tyrannical majorette in his high school marching band.

"What did you do with it?" he asked.

"With what?"

"The foot. The leg. Did you throw it out already?"

"We have sophisticated and sanitary methods of disposal—you needn't worry about that."

"No, I'm wondering if we can keep it."

"There's no chance for reattachment. I assure you the doctors tried every available means to save the limb."

"Right, right. I realize they had to hack it. But can we have it? The leg?"

For a moment Frances Rampling's expression became entirely unprofessional, with not just the forehead thing, but full wrinkle of her beaky nose. She replicated that face when she was on the stand. Although she had an orderly life, Frances had gotten into several catfights in high school. All involving a lot of fingernail.

Perhaps Jebediah wanted to articulate a few more wishes, or maybe thought he could keep the foot pickled in a jar, like those two headed babies in that Philadelphia oddity museum. When both Thaddeus J. Ebbers and the prosecuting attorney asked him to explain, he just said, "It belongs to Edith. I thought she would want it back." The wet shine in his eyes produced sympathy in the courtroom, but not from Frances Rampling with her passion for cleanliness and rules. Frances clicked her pointy tongue and said the word "unsanitary" five times in three sentences.

Edith seemed smaller under the scrutiny of the hospital's harsh lights. Jebediah had the foresight to buy his bride an orange soda.

"Thank you, darling," she said shyly. "Is it terribly ugly?" She pulled back the crisp white sheet, uncovering a mess of bandages where her left knee used to continue.

"You are lovely. Just lovely." Jebediah kissed as close to the bandages as he dared. "Besides, your shoes will last twice as long."

After all the emotional moments, the whole courtroom cracked up at this, releasing the tensions and bated breath. When Jebediah finally drove Edith away, he had already been released from County lockup on his own recognizance, and he acted as if he didn't miss that foot that got him arrested a bit.

The real acquittal came at the liquor store, two months after the "not-guilty" allowed Jebediah back to fixing up the house for his (future) bride. On this Tuesday afternoon, with heavy air that smelled like snow, Jeb brought a bottle of Canadian whiskey to the counter, "for medicinal purposes." His eyes shone in with his old sly humor, and his longer-than-ever hair flopped over his forehead comically.

"So how's everything going, Jebediah? How's Edith?" Al Murray asked while sliding the whiskey into a brown paper bag. We waited for Jebediah to talk, outside of the official context. He and Edith had retreated to Turner's Point with only the occasional quick grocery sweeps.

"Well, I know now that I didn't need that foot," he said to Al Murray, knowing full well that three other people were in the store, not to mention that Al Murray has a mouth the size of Seneca Caverns.

"Why's that?" Al asked for us all.

"We had enough good luck for any two people I guess," Jebediah said, bringing back that laughter that so many of us feel in the base of our spines. And then, no thanks to Thaddeus J. Ebbers Esq., we forgave them both.

A Girlfriend's

Guide to

Amy Fisher

Amy Fisher jokes never go out of style in New Jersey. With that unflagging optimism, Amy's gun butts right up against her romantic problems, her sweet Daddy-age mechanic and his there-first bride. Amy marches up to the door, rings the bell, and when the wife opens wide, well, we all know the story. Instead of a proposal, a conviction—plus those magazines, the jokes and three made-for-TV movies.

> Knock Knock.
> Who's there?
> Amy Fisher
> Amy F—
> BANG!!!!!

Funny, but a real friend has to speak up. Men you think have good intentions have a blade visible in the corner of their eyes. No joke.

Goin'

Nowhere

Oh, oh, are we gonna fly
Down into the easy chair.
—Bob Dylan, "You Ain't Goin' Nowhere"

The flat metal nowhere of the Atlantic spreads ahead and Atlantic City spreads behind. It took the tickets, the raffle, the spread, above the line, below the line. Hot tailgate cools in salt air and doors click. Our brides wait and we said *it's okay, baby,* telling them about that sweet chair. It's coming. We just can't lose that Genghis Khan thing, that children in every corner of the kingdom thing and that stay up all night long without blinking thing. Just a few hours ago a lady with sleepy eyes and blue spangles had an extra-long grip on the brown bottle. The flat-white ferry runs so early we're still shaking night off, blinking away lights and spangles. Breathing smoke into salt air. The seagulls wheeling and dealing pull us up, keep us steady—the world thumps, but only if we know where to press our ears.

What's Going Down at the Electric Radish?

In the corner of my eye, something flashed. I was jittery, having swallowed only coffee and birth control since waking. Quickly, I turned toward the green flash. A granny-smith-green tandem bicycle disappeared into an alley behind Kinkos. I swerved the car and my recently rented copy of *Xanadu* slid from the front seat.

How many of these bikes could there be in a medium-sized town?

The helmeted couple had to be Sonia and Travis. Perhaps the tandem bike had some other environmental pluses—less metal than two bikes, less overall worms squished—but they bought it in that twinned relationship stage where one would keep glancing at the bathroom while the other was taking a shower. Sonia/Sunny made a joke about Travis's gas (too much tofu can get twisted), but in that voice new mothers use to complain about changing diapers, the mock-annoyance belying a conviction that their baby's butt actually smells adorable.

I would have tried to follow them down the alley but the path was too skinny for my Volvo. Had they seen me?

Sunny hadn't called me for two years. If she and Travis were still in town and had just managed to avoid me for all this time, I wanted to know. This gymnast I had an exhausting three-week affair with years ago still turns up everywhere. After the novelty of his hard protean body wore off, the common ground spun away. I had to exchange pleasantries with this flexible fellow at least once a week in coffee shops, drugstores and the occasional spoken word performance. But I never *ever* ran into my friend Sonia—now Sunny. This had to be because she had finally joined the Peace Corps. Perhaps they don't have phones in remote areas of Rwanda.

The alternative clenched in my stomach.

The day after the tandem sighting, I drove to the Electric Radish, a fashionable and expensive grocery store with exemplary politics. I never shopped there, but Travis worked as a shelver there last I saw him.

I stepped through the energy-efficient lobby (artfully adorned with multi-colored citrus fruits) and began my search.

"Are you looking for someone?" a blond man stacking leeks asked. His voice growled sweetly in a way I felt in my stomach. Then I noticed his t-shirt emblazoned with a yellow string of nonsense words.

Sim the skater, who had never called.

Last time I ran into him he had one of those healthy-hiker ponytails, but now sported short hair and a narrow goatee meant for thoughtful rubbing.

"Hey, Sim. I'm looking for my best friend. Well, I mean, for her boyfriend who used to work here. She stopped calling. I think I made him angry. I guess her, too," I said in a rush of revelation. Sim smelled like onions and salt, and maybe that made me emotional in his presence. He ran his hand down my arm and hummed sympathetically.

"What is his name?" he asked.

"Travis."

"Was he up in arms about food additives?"

"Yes, exactly. Tall, reddish sideburns. Do you know him?"

"Nope. But I sure know the type. Chances are he doesn't

work here anymore."

Perhaps Sim was wrong, oblivious to new hairstyles or different shifts. But when we asked the dreadlocked employee on a stepladder arranging plums in a ceiling-mister haze, he told us that Travis was long gone. "Yep," Sim said. "The buyout rumors must be true. I would really love to be near you sometime again." He gave me a squeeze, gently toothed the top of my ear, and said he needed to "go finish the dig."

Whatever that meant.

Once, before Travis decided that I was more insidious and molecularly damaging than pesticide, they set me up on a blind date with one of his Electric Radish coworkers. My date "hadn't had a morsel of red meat or a drop of dairy" in fifteen years, and it absolutely showed. For three tedious hours, the double date consisted of discussions about what bleached flour and dairy do to your colon. In molecular detail.

I kept trying to make jokes with Sonia, perhaps to lure her away for a beer. But she was on a yeast-free diet and kept abreast of the conversation.

And there he was, in bulk grains at the Electric Radish, his hands stuffed with organic greens. Maybe he knew something. His name was a self-conscious abbreviation of some sort. Toph? Xander?

"Hey, buddy. Remember me?" I asked, quickly swallowing the last of the free Quinoa cereal sample.

The guy blinked rapidly and nearly tottered off his stool. He needed protein, and fast.

"Have you heard from Travis lately?" I chirped, not wanting to let on that I was so far removed from the Sonia/Travis loop. Maybe my former blind date would let it slip

"Well. Lately. Well. Not in a few weeks," he said.

"Are they still in town?"

"Well, of course. Don't you—"

"Gotta go," I said, before he snapped some connection or another. Our last parting had been abrupt, too. Somehow my ignorance about the danger of genetically engineered food had worked both my date and Travis into a froth. They had piles of statistics and studies on the tips of their tongues. My sarcasm was as much a cover for ignorance as a belittling of danger. How did they find out all of these things, about how corn used to have fewer, but inordinately better, kernels? Where did they get all of their synchronized information? Some kind of *Anarchist's Cookbook*, except with real recipes?

Sonia and I had our own conspiracy theories, first about the ingredients of Mountain Dew and later about birth control's control of the female mind. The whole regulation of a woman's cycle, making sure that there are no sharp spikes or dips, has to be a kind of emotional manipulation. Not to mention that birth control works by creating an artificial pregnancy; isn't this exactly as the bigwigs would want us all? Now the pill comes in the "credit card" model, just like Business Barbie and Doctor Barbie. Breaking out of the old stereotypes that produced the pastel pink "compact," which dispensed candy-colored birth control in a cleverly-disguised-as-make-up container. Because now, of course, Barbie needs a job, not just a made-up face to compliment her chemically-created infertility. Sonia and I had read *A Wrinkle in Time* in seventh grade, soon after our parents had finished whispering about Watergate, and had been big on government-control conspiracy theories ever since.

"I will never let the government give me chemicals to control me," Sonia said, linking her pinky with mine.

"I will never let the government give me chemicals to control me," I said. "Or carry a briefcase." After my pregnancy scare the first year of college, we both shifted position on the pill. We both decided to *take* it, but never let it win.

On the date, I found out that American bodies don't decay after death, due to preservatives, and American people are apolitical because of bleached flour. My suspicious nature would have felt more of an alliance if I could have stopped obsessing about the irony of my blind date's breath like rotting meat.

"They drug the American people," Travis informed me. "The people who buy individually packaged snack foods and order dinner at McDonald's. They know how to get us, they know how to get it *into* us." Sparkly sweat glittered on Travis's upper lip when he discussed food fascism. Maybe Sonia sensed that I really did not like her boyfriend and that started the rift between us. He was very handsome, with a rock-climber's bodily efficiency, no additives or preservatives. Also he doted on Sonia, who he never called anything but Sunny, both emotionally and physically, laying claim to her with his hand, or draping his leg over her knee. In high school, Sonia rarely got asked out, being the shy one.

"I never know what to say to boys," she would laugh as we whispered to each other. Afterwards we would go to my house and eat cookie dough from a fat plastic sleeve. With our hands. We would just dig right in.

A few weeks after my fruitless Sonia-search at the Electric Radish, Sim the skater left a voicemail saying he would be stopping by at two in the morning. I perked up a bit. He was strange but adorable. Recently, in my cultivation of a professional life, I found myself without much male companionship. Or male companionship of the most sterile kind, the ones with pink button-up shirts and combed back hair. Sim the grown-up skater was cute enough to be in an adult boy band while still seeming intelligent. The guys at work talked about the stock market as if it were interesting. We had met when I knocked him off his skateboard with my grocery cart. I made a quick turn by the Safeway exit, where he was performing all manner of tricks. We both could have been watching more closely.

"Simple," he said, proffering his hand. "That's my name, Simple."

"Ah," I replied. "Nickname?"

"Nope. Call me Sim."

A car drove by and someone yelled out the window, "You are supporting SLAVEWAY! Capitalist pigs!"

"When did grocery shopping become so political?" I blamed additives and preservatives at least in part for the fact that I could not seem to find my best friend. Or, more accurately, that she did not want me to find her.

"You don't know the half of it," Sim said, and drew his finger down the back of my neck. I stopped thinking about Sunny/Sonia and Travis's grocery agenda and noticed that this adult skate rat had delicious legs beneath his torn shorts.

"Anything I can do to make up for hitting you with my cart?" I asked in what I hoped was a playfully provocative tone.

"Nope," he said. "But maybe I'll call you sometime."

Which wasn't of course for months and months.

I ordered Chinese delivery while I waited for Sim to stop by. Why two in the morning?

I had fallen asleep during *Xanadu* and was dreaming of roller derbies.

He breezed in and whipped the conversation around all kinds of kinks and bends. Sadly, for the first four hours, he stayed on his side of the couch. Then he made some politically correct comment, so I had to ask:

"Are you a vegan?"

"Oh, no. Then I wouldn't be able to eat pork rinds." He eyes gleamed. "Do you have any dietary restrictions?"

"Heavens, no!" I answered. "When I don't feel like cooking I just lick lard off my fingers." Lack of sleep made me giddy and slightly intoxicated. And then Sim was perched on my lap, delicately licking my fingers. After my fingers, my toes. When he finally kissed me, I tasted the fine fuzz of nicotine, salt, and MSG.

At some point, the adult skater jumped up.

"What time is it?" I asked, allover disoriented.

"I have to show friends around town at nine," Sim said.

Sim slipped downstairs. His voice wafted back up right before the door squeezed shut. "Be sure you call me," he said. "I never text."

The hospital. Maybe Sonia still worked at the hospital. The ER nurses were not supposed to get personal calls, but perhaps Sonia would forgive me when she realized how determined I was to patch things up. Maybe being called Sunny would make her bright and upbeat. But no. The southern accent on the phone assured me that Sonia hadn't worked there in over a year and besides, the ER nurses were not supposed to take personal calls.

I tried to call Sim. The message changed each time, never quite catching his voice. These messages combined snippets of songs, jingles and strange laughter. I finally texted and got a pumpkin emoji back.

With the early spring, the protesters gathered in front of grocery stores daily. More and more placards detailing the destruction of rainforests and human tissue. Additives, preservatives, bleached flour, pesticides. The throng of them became larger and longer, bleeding into the parking lot.

BOVINE GROWTH HORMONE MAKES LITTLE GIRLS MENSTRUATE AT AGE FIVE!! a sign proclaimed.

As Sonia eased into being a vegetarian she would tell me about the terrible conditions and Frankensteinian measures they used to bring meat to the table, with some even growing shivering chickens with no feathers to pluck.

As this new person Sunny became more and more enmeshed in her relationship with Travis, she called less and less and lost more and more weight. Travis insisted that they eat their vegetables raw, so that the nutrients were not "tortured out of them." When they walked, she twined her long fingers in his.

Right before Sonia and Travis disappeared, I tried to have a conversation with Sonia about my recent confusion with the gymnast. Like the old days. But when I narrated, using my hands to illustrate some of the more technical maneuvers, her eyes never seemed to focus.

"You can't trust your own moods if you're eating their foods," Sonia said in her public voice, ignoring my private revelations. Travis appeared at her side and patted her shoulder.

"That's the truth, Sunny," he said. What if "Sunny" didn't fit her? She was a goth girl at heart, a Sylvia Plath fan, Smiths-loving, un-Sunny gal if ever the clouds did gather.

I borrowed a cigarette just to be contrary. Travis shook his head. "It's so easy to fight a war when so many march right into the slaughter."

For the next few months, I tried my hand at racquetball. I lacked graceful large-motor coordination, but it felt like really a productive use of aggression. My legs tired easily and my thoughts spun with caffeine, so I needed new routines. Plus, any exercise made me feel less guilty about what I ate. Four button-up fellows from my office played on a regular rotation, and they let me join. On my walk home from the courts, a bright red flyer blew across my path. I chased it into a parking lot.

Just as I managed to grab the paper, someone covered my eyes with chapped hands. I grabbed the wrists.

"Sim?" I guessed. I was right, of course, and probably identified him faster by remembering his wrists than if I had taken in his new, long, religiously-bushy beard. He skated around me in a happy circle.

"Why didn't you call?"

I gave him a hug and then shook my finger at him. "I called and texted."

"Oh, I share a phone with my skater roommate. Probably his fault." Sim's beard was surprisingly red. "I can't wait to see you again but I'm late for work," he said.

The paper flapped in my hand as Sim skated away. The pamphlet proclaimed: RED #48 IS A FORM OF GOVERNMENT CONTROL.

Beneath this headline, the science was spelled out. Red #48 winds its way through the body like the fifth-level Centipede in the eponymous video game. Figuring and reconfiguring in your body. And unless your immune system really sticks to its guns, it moves on the next level before a body can really break it down. No one knows what exactly it does in there (although perhaps Travis does by now) but corpses have been found with brilliant scarlet interiors, still a shade of Red #48 and so pumped full of preservatives that they barely decay.

This was Sonia's fight, to keep her body intact from the onslaught of chemicals and controls. Me, I still put Nair on my legs, unquestioning as to what could possibly make each hair flake off with just a touch. Don't look a gift poison in the mouth. Sure, Travis was over the top, but Sonia chose him instead of me. My lifestyle made coexistence impossible. My head hurt, but then again all I had eaten before playing racquetball was a glossy danish full of bleached flour and processed sugar.

•

Maybe what I needed was to refocus my energies. Not go full on vegan or anything, but get healthy, take kickboxing. And so, one afternoon, I found myself fruit shopping at the Electric Radish, deliberately avoiding the bulk grains section.

I stood in front of an apple display, where the jeweled fruit rose in an architecture; when I pulled an apple from this pile, it seemed quite an accomplishment. The surface shone with what might have been Red #48. I tapped my fingernails three times against the exoskeleton. Smooth as candy.

A woman wearing purple veils over a pale face set back deeply in her brown hood pressed close against me. She was either a belly-dancer, deeply religious, or a guru. Or all of the above—a devout, dancing, wise woman. She was something familiar. In our supercharged political climate, I wanted to protect her from the terrible people who freaked when women covered their heads. I wanted to uphold her rights, to support her causes. But then I breathed her in and I almost dropped my apple. Garlic, with an undertone of lilacs.

"You need to leave this store *right now* for your own safety," she said and gave me a strong shove. Beneath the preponderance of gauzy cloth came a voice like Sonia's. I stumbled a step or two, steadied myself on some well-stacked kiwis, and glanced back. She had disappeared.

Winding my way out of the store, I saw a familiar t-shirt hovering over the individually packaged snack foods. I grabbed the sleeve of Sim's shirt, and whirled him around. "We have to get out of here," I said, and noted that his hair was Easter-egg blue. Thank goodness for that t-shirt.

To his credit, Sim did not hesitate. Whistling wetly, but not saying a word, he followed me through electric doors and down the sidewalk. We sat beneath a tree at a safe distance from the store. The automatic doors slid open and closed, open and closed.

Hypnotized, we watched those doors and shared the shiny apple I had inadvertently shoplifted.

Twelve Dancing Princesses in a Honkytonk

"What's with their shoes?" Mr. Duke pressed his fingertips against his shiny forehead. He sucked a ragged breath and swept his hand towards Elsie's feet. "Why are your shoes so dirty?"

"Gardens. You know we love to walk in the gardens." Elsie stood slightly taller than the bald headmaster, and her posture made her even taller. Despite the blue smudges beneath her firefly eyes, we all found her so beautiful it was difficult to look right at her. "Exercise helps the mind. I think it helps us score well."

Behind her, three other members of the Dirty Dozen nodded. What could Mr. Duke say? These girls with ruined shoes kept our numbers, the ones that they published on card stock paper to give to parents and the board, so high, despite Nelson Tallington (of the Hartford Tallingtons) and his obscene flatulence during any testing session.

Elsie and the girls behind her looked much like us from the ankles up. But their shoes had scuffs beyond bushes, mud from somewhere unlike the gentle brown Beloeil flowerbeds.

The rest of us at Beloeil were hidden there, tucked away in a big stone building by parents tired of whining. Of calls from principals. Of finding pot in backpacks. Of dealing with the unwieldy facts of teenagers.

But not Michael, and not the twelve.

Thirteen students at Beloeil *choose* our thin mattresses

and thick hallways. One was a pale boy who hated the seaside privilege of his New Jersey homelife and the other twelve were the Dirty Dozen, locals gifted a "world class opportunity."

The scholarship girls. The Dozen. A gaggle of jealous young heiresses came up with the name, but we never meant it as an insult.

We complained and rolled our eyes about the palatial prison with its well-manicured grounds. When we did, Michael nodded sympathetically.

"I agree the chicken tastes like tires," he said. "But the rest isn't so bad."

Twelve girls raised our profile and our score averages. Brilliance and those dark-but-light eyes. The Dozen's families actually lived in the post-mining natural splendor populated with human poverty that surrounded Beloeil. The rest of us only visited for the school year.

Our families paid the massive monthly check to civilize us. They whispered the word to each other when our various troubles came to light, expulsions or new piercings.

"Beloeil," they hissed, with a firm nod. "It's lovely."

The humming made us crazy. We all wanted to find secrets of the scholarship girls, and most of all press up against one of them.

If you walked up behind one, totally quiet, you might hear them humming.

"I think it's honkytonk," one of us said and the rest of us took those voodoo words to heart. Honkytonk. We didn't know honkytonk in our various cities. We called fiddles violins.

But if the Dozen loved it, we could too. We tried to hum along.

They never studied because they never had to. We watched

with *Crime and Punishment* during mandated work time, and the Russian nicknames butterflied on quick pages. These girls knew from moral dilemmas. They took tests that made us all look smarter and finished reading books so fast we all felt dumber. They clumped together even when the daughter of that oil company exec tempted to the fight (soon quelled by Elsie's quiet offer to take it outside), or that son of Wall Street offered companionship (soon quelled by the small sleepy smiles of all them).

Few images burned like Elsie's yellow-in-the-center eyes. We pretended her eyes didn't glow in study sessions or distract us across the quad. Bunny Ilswich (of the Springfield Ilswiches) couldn't stop staring at Elsie's eyes, since her mad love for the girl went beyond our garden-variety desire. Poor Bunny teared up if Elsie glanced her way, and her hand shook when she turned pages in the textbook. She wrote poem after terrible poem in the margins of her math homework. We pondered whether her mother's drinking contributed to her over-the-moonies.

Beloeil shaped our daily life, but our past steeped us in the cocktail of genetics and such.

We whispered that the Dozen, like most locals, were some sort of Indian, some sort of tribe. How did anyone actually end up in the middle of these forested hills, softened with age, full of mines and sinkholes? We were from cities, from far away success stories. Did their connection (to history, to each other) change their eyes and dirty their shoes?

"You're telling me that no one can fix this shoe problem?" Mr. Duke loved those paintings of women with pastel umbrellas, and he loved our uniformed conformity. On Parent Weekend, just one week away, he wanted our rich, fed-up parents to observe our neat sameness and visible compliance. He had proudly hand-picked the Dirty Dozen from interviews and test scores.

But their shoes.

Though their uniforms looked just like ours, they held their mouths differently, humming, and their shoes were scuffed past recognition. They were birds held by the stone ceilings, but only until the after dinner bell rang.

Where their shoes sunk into the earth, where they migrated, we had no idea. We never saw their eyes flash or their hands flutter before they disappeared.

"I can follow them," Michael said.

"Do you have a tracking device?" one of us asked.

"Do you have a lock-picking kit like that kid that got kicked out of Groton?"

Michael smiled small. "I have the power of invisibility." We hadn't really noticed him before. His hair was a hard to describe not-brown, not-blond. His skin was blondish/brownish too. He had the kind of features that looked a lot like anyone else's, and he reminded everyone of someone, but we couldn't think of who it was.

And he really could be invisible, we found out. He decided to follow the youngest, Lina. We grabbed Michael's worksheets, turned in his homework and even said "present" in history, because our teacher would never notice.

"I keep feeling like someone's behind me," Lina said.

"That's what she said," another of the twelve responded.

Michael's ability to slip through cracks fit beside the Dozen's ability to dodge the walls. Maybe he should have been born in Appalachia—he certainly understood it better than we did, used to our sharp corners and discordant noises. Darkness beneath softness.

We never quite got the story right. We never quite

understood Michael's descriptions of dark once-mining passages beneath the school, the lanterns, and the pressing darkness. When he told us about the shack pressed full of people, dancing somewhere in the middle of nowhere—we felt something move but we couldn't hear the music. We tried to see the Dirty Dozen stomping and spinning on wood floors.

Elsie stood to sing a song that Michael couldn't fit to words. With the clinking of breakfast around us, he tried to tell us that honkytonk song, but all he managed was a staccato buzz.

He didn't follow them again, because now Nina saw him. On movie night, Michael sat next to Nina, and during *North by Northwest* they held hands beneath a black and white Mount Rushmore. Some nights, his thin mattress was empty, though none of us saw him leave.

We could have told Mr. Duke. Maybe we could have negotiated with Elsie, gotten a dance or two in return or at least some homework help. Instead, we waited, because soon we might get to be invisible.

Fair

States

Aunt Rainy arrived in a faded Volkswagen, with red eyes and unrestrained hair. Nothing made Reuben Murphy happier than the fact that he sat atop the tractor when she pulled up the dirt road. She stepped out of the car and the sunlight made her hair look liquid. Reuben shaded his eyes. A pale moon of belly was visible when she stretched her arms above her head.

"Hey, guys," she said. "Check out Reuben."

Reuben quickly pulled the white papery mask down to his chin so that his aunt could see his grin. With his new allergy pills, Reuben could drive the tractor above the fields of his discontent, but only while wearing a medical mask. His mother got a whole box at cost from a high school friend who now worked down at the hospital. The masks diluted the farm's tangy smell—which was actually small irritating particles (pollen, hair, manure) worming their way into Reuben's body, coating his throat, catching in his nose. He was allergic to the Midwest.

Reuben's three little sisters ran toward their aunt, shrieking like crows. The twins (Anna and Amy, who Reuben called "Annamy" since they were exactly the same) came from the barn, while baby Angel (who walked and talked but was never called anything but "baby Angel") pulled away from her mother in front of the house and ran toward the round yellow car.

"Baby Angel, don't you fall down now," Iris Murphy said as the little girl bounced along on chubby legs. Iris refused to run, walking very deliberately down the porch steps. Five children in ten years made Iris Murphy look far older than thirty-five and made her husband work far harder than other men his age. Each of Iris and Big Den Murphy's kids worked; even baby Angel fed the chickens. The twin girls Anna and Amy did the rest of chicken duty and much of the milking; the oldest, Denny, had moved up to horses and heavier field handing, but Reuben's rotation included mostly indoor duties. Until the latest visit to town, where the pills were stapled into a white paper bag and handed to his mother.

"Well, honey, these could change everything," she said, pulling his thin shoulders close in to her big, soft body.

Iris loved her boy in a mask, made him her favorite child, told him her secrets, and for this the other kids didn't like him at all. Adults, however, loved Reuben, the most polite of all his mother's children, and plus, he had the allergies. Raging, made-for-air-conditioning allergies. His brother used a pitchfork, and the girls chased chickens while Reuben watched all of this from the other side of the kitchen window, thick, slightly-waved glass above the double sinks. On the other side, his brother's darkening limbs blurred across the farmyard. With small eyes and a near-constant sunburn, Denny spent very little time in the house, always running out to do chores or wander in the adjacent woods. Occasionally in inclement weather he would stay inside and shoot darts with Reuben, but lately the weather had been fine. Turning fifteen, Denny convinced their father to allow him to have his bangs hang down into his eyelashes, giving him a flirty look and protecting him a bit more from the Midwestern sun. Reuben thought that Denny probably did it to hide the angry zits that had begun to crowd his forehead, rather than to block the light.

"Are you a doctor, or a cowboy?" Denny asked from beneath his long hair when he saw Reuben prepare for his first day driving. Reuben fiddled with the ignition, even though he had to wait for his father to turn the tractor on.

"He looks like a doctor," one of the twins said.

"But he's a big bad cowboy, like with a mask to rob someone," the other twin said.

"No, he thinks he's the big bad *plowboy*," Denny replied with a snort.

"Yee-Haw!" a twin said.

"Make that bronco buck!"

"You look funny," baby Angel said. She was only three and even she joined in the mockery. Reuben didn't even find baby Angel bearable anymore. But they were just jealous. Even Denny hardly ever got to drive the tractor and he was almost old enough for a driver's license. No matter what, sitting astride the hot metal must be mockable or else they all would wish for Reuben's watery eyes. This was what he wished for, an outside job, one on the other side of the glass. When he stood squirting water on the dishes or fitting rings onto sticky jars, he would watch the others dart across the thick kitchen window. Now he wished only for them to shut their traps.

When Reuben's father trudged out of the barn to start the tractor, everyone hushed. Big Den never said much, but his stare could melt peanut butter.

Aunt Rainy blew the hair from her forehead and dropped her blue dufflebag. "How did you stand it, Iris?"

"Stand what, Lorraine?"

"It's Rainy."

"Stand what?"

"The deathly silence in that house. The oppressive shit."

"Rainy! The children."

"Hey, kids!" Their aunt turned away from her sister's

disapproval. "Anyone saved some hugs for a Rainy day?"

The three little girls hurled themselves against Aunt Rainy's long purple skirt and spicy-smelling hair. She hugged the twins, picked up little Baby Angel and kissed her on the nose. Denny hung back, and Reuben debated whether or not he should dismount. He decided that forfeiting the hug might be worth it to remain in his position on high. His aunt smiled more than anyone he knew, even now that she had just finished her "disastrous affair," as Reuben's mother informed him.

Whatever that meant.

"Look at you up there," Rainy said, grabbing his hand and kissing it, like a suited man in the movies. He could smell her, a combination of fruit and Christmas. He wanted to say something wonderful.

But Rainy looked beyond him, toward the far field. "Hey Denny," she said over Reuben's hand. "Aren't you quite the man?" Reuben's arm dropped back onto his overalls and he saw his brother push his pointy chin forward as he walked toward the tractor. "How old are you now?"

"Fifteen."

"Ah. Old enough!" Aunt Rainy replied. "I like that new hair."

Behind her little sister, their mother clicked her tongue. "Let's get your bag upstairs, Lorraine. Big Den, you want to help us?"

After their mother herded Aunt Rainy inside and their father followed with the colorful bag, Denny pressed a long weed up towards Reuben's cheek. In the back of his throat, Reuben felt a familiar thickening. Everything to do with breathing warped and his breath began to whistle. He steered the tractor slightly off course as he fumbled for his inhaler in the overall's front pocket.

Either the unsteady path or Reuben's shoulders spiked down over the steering wheel got his father's attention. The man sprinted over, stopped the tractor, and stood with his hand on his son's back until Reuben's breath steadied. Reuben's vision blurred until he felt his inhaler reshape his throat.

He just hoped that Aunt Rainy didn't see.

Big Den stayed beside Reuben and walked him back into the house.

"Back already?" Iris asked, and then she saw Reuben's dangling mask and his swollen eyes. She grabbed his cheeks and looked into the pained red puff around his eyelids. He couldn't even muster disappointment when Iris said, "Whatever's growing out there is just not good for you Reuben. You need to stay in and help me tomorrow."

Reuben pursed his lips and stared at his dusty shoes (which he would have to remember to not put near his bed.) His mother pushed his hair gently away from his blotchy forehead and pulled him into her soft chest for a hug. With a quick intake of breath, Reuben turned away.

"Hey, bud, great driving out there," Aunt Rainy said. She hugged him so hard that he could feel her breasts pushing against the buttons of his overalls. He felt light-headed again, with air swollen in his chest and his eyes filling. He loved his aunt, but she may also have had cat hair on her coat.

"Big Den doesn't have much to say does he?" said Aunt Rainy.

"He is not a man for idle chatter," said Reuben's mother, giving the potato a particularly malicious swipe with the peeler.

"Doesn't that get lonely?"

"Lorraine, I have five children and a farm. I'm not lonely."

"That's not what I mean. And only Mom calls me Lorraine. Is that really the company you want to keep?"

"Why are you so mad at them?"

"Why did you get married at seventeen, Iris?" Rainy

countered.

"Because I was in love."

"Right." Rainy walked away without drying the rest of the lettuce.

"What do you know about Christian love?" Iris mumbled. Reuben heard her (though he was not sure what "Christian" had to do with love), but his aunt's long strides were already pushing through long grass of the front lawn. Denny was supposed to mow it yesterday.

Reuben walked in the kitchen. His mother's face shifted into a new shape when she saw him. "Oh, good!"

Luckily, his siblings or Aunt Rainy couldn't hear. "I need some help chopping all of this," his mother continued. "I'm far too sentimental to cut onions, and we all know that Rainy is no help at all in the kitchen."

Reuben went to get the saltines. Although his eyes watered at the slightest provocation from pollen, dander, hay, dust, he could handle onions. He popped a cracker into his mouth. Grandma Murphy taught him this trick, to absorb the smell. He balanced the cracker delicately between his lips and pulled the onions onto the wooden cutting board.

"How in the world can she be twenty-six, still without her own apartment, still unmarried and worst of all, unable to cook?"

The cracker excused Reuben's silence. His mother wiped her hands on her jeans and pulled out the potatoes.

As Reuben began to chop, she made a phone call. "Well, she had to come. No…not because of that. I think Daddy caught them at it. So no more free rent at the old homestead. She said she will pay us a nominal fee to stay here, though I'm not sure how long it will last…She's totally despondent, I'm sure. A business associate…of course married…"

Without meaning to, Reuben pressed his lips together so hard that the cracker broke and scattered onto linoleum. He had watched enough daytime television with his mother when he was home sick to know about affairs. Nudity, cars, accusations. But that wasn't Aunt Rainy, not screaming and naked. He would brush his aunt's tears away and murmur that everything would be okay, as long as she stayed for a long time. A very long time. Reuben felt his vision blur a bit as the thick onion fumes moved past his crackerless mouth and into his eyes.

"Well, what else could I do?" his mother said into the phone. "It's only Christian. She is my little sister, after all."

"Wow! Look at this guy cook. I know nothing of such mysteries." Aunt Rainy slid into the kitchen on bare feet. Reuben flushed until he saw Denny standing behind her. Denny found Reuben's kitchen skill hilarious.

"I'll go pick some flowers for the table," Rainy said. She and Denny kept walking onto the broad porch, and down the steps.

"How is she ever going to find a man—one that's not already married—if she can't cook anything?" Iris Murphy whispered to the phone.

"Mom, Dad says I can try the tractor again tomorrow since he has to do the west field," Reuben said that night at dinner. He knew his father wouldn't bring it up, but Iris would be more likely to agree if her husband sat beside her carving his chop into small squares.

"Sweetheart, I don't know if that's a good idea. Remember the last time," Iris said.

"Yeah, but Denny was messing around. This time he knows not to mess around."

Denny bent his head low, but looked at Reuben from beneath his bangs. He slowly opened his mouth to show Reuben the violent mixture of pork and green beans between his teeth.

"Ewwww," said Baby Angel. "Denny didn't close his mouth."

"Bad enough you cannot talk to your own family, Denny," Iris said. "At least you could let us see your eyes."

Denny slowly lifted his bangs on the back of his hand and pushed his eyeballs forward. "Happy?" Denny said.

"Oh, I'm always happy," said Iris. She glanced at her husband, who chewed and stared down at his salad. Rainy covered her mouth with a napkin and a suspiciously laughy sound leaked from behind it.

"So, we cannot wait until church night at the state fair. Are you boys going to come to the Gemma May Harmony concert with us?" Iris said. Gemma May Harmony, an aging gospel singer with huge hair and spangled cowgirl outfits, was considered a good influence. The boys that hung out by the dart games were not.

"No. I don't like that Harmony lady and her screechy singing. I heard that wasn't her real name," Denny said.

"Well, I never heard that it wasn't," his mother replied.

"I heard that too," said Aunt Rainy. "I think her real name is Ima Butt."

Aunt Rainy and Denny cracked up. Reuben giggled, but then wondered if Rainy and Denny had worked this joke out in advance, in one of their private conversations. He stopped giggling and finished his milk.

"She serves the Lord, and it seems small to mock her," Iris said to her eldest son without glancing at her laughing sister. She cleared the plates.

The 4-H club was sponsoring a dance after the youth division livestock judging. If Reuben just stayed away from the animal tents with fur and hay suspended in the thick air, and as long as he didn't dance with some girl who spent all afternoon showing her Appaloosa without ever washing her hands, Reuben could step into the streamers.

•

Right inside the open door of the bathroom, Aunt Rainy swiped candy-colored deodorant into the dark hollow of her armpit. Without meaning to, Reuben stopped and leaned his shoulder against the wall. Denny strode down the hallway and stopped right behind Reuben.

"I didn't know I had an audience." Aunt Rainy peered at them through the medicine cabinet mirror.

"Sorry," Reuben mumbled.

"We need to know a bit more about grooming," Denny said. He was even taller than Reuben remembered. They all laughed, and Iris walked up the stairs.

"What's going on, some kind of party?"

"Oh, I think the boys have some questions about personal hygiene." Rainy laughed.

After Rainy shut the door to her room, Iris turned to her sons. "Aunt Rainy is fun to have around isn't she?"

Reuben recognized that this question held some kind of a trick, a secret code. "Sure," he said. Denny didn't say a thing.

"I'm glad to see she is looking better. She used to have such acne you know. I really lucked out in the skin department. Rainy still has a few blemishes around her jawline, but really it used to be quite angry." Their mother paused, as if to give her sons time to answer. "When we were girls, young like you two, I used to pray for her every day. Can you imagine that?"

Saturday, after the morning chores, Iris Murphy wrestled the girls into coats. "Rudy and Denny, we are going into town to get tickets for Gemma May Harmony. I'll bet anything she sells out. You should come with. Denny, we can take you down to the barber shop."

"Don't buy me a ticket. And I don't want a haircut, Mom," Denny said.

"You need one. You can't even see out from underneath it."

"Aunt Rainy likes my hair."

"Denny, I don't think you should use Aunt Rainy as some kind of hair judge." Their mother swiped a finger across Denny's cheek. "Her hair should be taken into consideration."

"Her hair is pretty."

"Her hair is a teenager's. Hippy hair. She doesn't cut it but once a year."

"Maybe you should cut your hair less, Mom."

"Like I want hair advice from someone who looks like a shoplifter."

Reuben ran after his mother.

"I don't want to go to the concert either," he said. He could just go straight to the dance. He didn't want to watch the woman hold those notes about Jesus for so long.

"But you love her music. We have the tape in the car."

"I know. But I think I just want to go to the dance."

Reuben saw his mother pause in front of the hall mirror, the one with built-in candleholders. She patted her tidy curls. She stepped back. She pulled one of her carefully permed locks down and held it close to her chin.

"Are you boys going to the big 4-H dance?" Aunt Rainy asked.

"The Round-Up," said Reuben.

"What?"

"Oh, that's their silly name for it," said Denny. "I'm not sure I'm into it." Reuben stared at his brother. Denny lit up at dances, since he could do all these robot moves and everyone would stand circle around him clapping.

"Why wouldn't you be into a dance, a Round-Up, full of teenage girls?" Aunt Rainy tilted her head, and brushed her hair behind her ear, all the while letting a slow smile widen her mouth.

"I'm into it," Reuben said.

"You know how teenage girls are," Denny said, as if the subject were tired.

"Well, I'm not a teenager anymore, young man. So maybe I don't." Aunt Rainy laughed.

"I'm sure you remember. They just all want a piece of you," Denny said.

"Maybe a piece of *you*," Rainy said, grabbing a handful of Denny's hip. The whites of Denny's eyes flashed for a moment beneath his hair. Then he started to laugh. Reuben slipped away.

Aunt Rainy would pick up little Baby Angel and fly her around the kitchen, but soon put her down. As soon as the twins started to fuss, Rainy would blow her hair out of her eyes and leave the room. But, it seemed to Reuben, she never got tired of Denny.

"I'm going for a walk," Aunt Rainy called each night after dinner. Iris would make a small sound of disbelief.

"She sure enjoys her nature walks," their mother said. "I think she is still smoking. All those studies, you would think she would know better." With his hands sweeping rhythmically over the wet dishes, Reuben looked at his mother's profile. Her thick arms lowered in the sinkful of soap, and she blinked her black lashes. Reuben could remember that his mother was still pretty, at least when Aunt Rainy was beside her. On her own, the pretty parts of Iris tended to fade into her serious expressions. Next to her sister, Iris stood up a little straighter purely to be competitive (since she was one inch taller but only if she remembered not to slouch). With Aunt Rainy nearby, the green of Iris's eyes became more visible, and the shape of her mouth almost looked like the breathy heart that was Rainy's lips. Any stranger could guess they were related if the features were considered side by side.

From a distance was another story.

Even Reuben's dad touched his mother more when Aunt

Rainy was staying. Maybe the sun hung around a little longer when Aunt Rainy was staying.

"How long will Aunt Rainy be here?" Reuben only looked at the plates.

"Until she figures out how to get a job and stop her scandalous behavior."

"What's scandalous behavior?" Reuben had a fairly good idea, but would have loved details.

Iris Murphy glanced behind her and leaned toward her youngest son. "It's when you do everything for your own pleasure, and damn everybody else."

The State Fair was as complicated as all its competing smells, of sweet dough and stinky dung. Flashy lights and rickety rides in constant movement, as roller coasters and adult-sized swings groaned and spun. Instead of staying in in their houses glowing blue with television, all the people spilled out.

The 4-H Round-Up would be in a tent, a place without definitive corners. Unlike school cafeteria dances, where the florescent lights of the cloakroom infected the darkness and allowed clear views of everyone trying to move their bodies closer to each other.

At the last school dance, a girl, Lucinda, who never noticed him at school (except perhaps when he collapsed at the pep rally) walked over and pulled Reuben's hand from his pocket. As she led him onto the dance floor Reuben managed to say, "Would you like to dance?" Instead of answering, she pressed her breasts right into his collarbones (since she stood a good six inches taller) and began to sway. She pulled away near the end of the song when the chorus repeated twice in a row. Reuben felt a moment of panic; the song wasn't really over—was she that eager to escape? But instead of removing the pressure of her thighs from his groin, she angled her head down.

Frozen moments ride on.

Her lips lowered to his cheekbone, brushed back into his hair and rose again. By the time Reuben gathered himself together the song really was over, and she had pulled herself away. When Lucinda walked towards the growing cluster of girls ,she never turned back. Reuben replayed that moment, each time tilting his face up at the right moment so that his lips would meet hers. If he had the chance again, this time he would make sure everything lined up.

On the car ride home from that last school dance, Reuben tried to envision the smooth sweep of his chin up to meet hers. Only slightly to the side so they would not crunch together. Lift the chin, tilt the head.

"What is wrong with you? Are you trying to catch flies?" Denny asked.

"Shut up."

That Monday at school, Reuben was ready, to tilt his head and lift his chin. He wondered if Lucinda would throw him up against the lockers in front of everyone, or pull him into the janitor's closet or behind the bleachers. This time he felt prepared, even to French kiss, though he would prefer to attempt this in one of the more remote locations. He looked for Lucinda everywhere. He stood by the door waiting and when she finally walked in, three abreast with her friends, he croaked out "hi" but she did not pause. They had not spoken since.

At the State Fair Round-up, Reuben would meet lips, tilt his chin. He would win Lucinda one of those stuffed animals for her to carry around.

•

That Saturday night, Reuben wore the blue shirt that Aunt Rainy had deemed "adorable." He took his extra allergy pills, and felt the fluttery energy from the double dose. His mother, father, and three little sisters had piled into the car two hours before, to eat at the hot dog bake before the Gemma May Harmony show. Denny convinced their mother that the boys should ride with Aunt Rainy later. Iris had asked Reuben which car he wanted, and although Reuben liked the idea of getting there early and practicing trying to win the tossing games, he knew that arriving in Aunt Rainy's rounded car would be much cooler. But now, he regretted his decision. Did they leave him? Aunt Rainy and his brother were nowhere to be found and Reuben paced around the house and porch, looking into the darkening distance for a sign of them running apologetically towards the house.

But Rainy's car still sat behind the barn.

Finally Reuben broke down and called the neighbors. They told him to cut across the fields and they could fit him into their car. Very kind people, the Dawsons. Except that Reuben could no more cut across the field than he could French kiss a cat; his allergies wouldn't let him, even with the extra pill. Reuben kicked the barn cat out of the way. No, not kicked really—he just let his foot assist in the cat's forward motion, so that the animal would have no illusions about whose lap to never never visit, and whose legs to never never curl around.

His eyes burned.

He couldn't miss the new girls, the ones that would come from all over the state. This time, more than just Lucinda or his neighbors would be there, swaying and waiting to press up against Reuben, he just knew it. Those Round-up girls would have no idea that Reuben once threw up into his plastic cafeteria tray, or had that asthma attack at the pep rally. But even if it was just Lucinda who wanted to tilt her head and brush her hair behind her ear for him—that was enough.

If he could just get there.

Maybe his mother was right, maybe Aunt Rainy did have a "damn everyone else" attitude. Reuben had to get to the Dawson place before they drove off, just in case Aunt Rainy had completely forgotten. Maybe she and Denny had decided to go in the station wagon after all, to save on gas as Iris had suggested. Maybe no one remembered that Reuben was home, hopped up on extra allergy pills waiting for his chance to revisit the Lucindas.

He would have to borrow the tractor.

The moonlight turned the waving rows of corn the color of the sea, the pale yellow lighting up just a fraction of the daytime green. The stars created a clear separation between the sky and the sea of corn.

Reuben lifted his surgical mask to breath in an untainted breath of the night air. The path between the two fields led to the Dawson's driveway (which was only half-way there since the driveway wound through a wood and two more Dawson cornfields.)

Reuben worried at his slow progress, as the heavy wheels churned through the dirt, and hoped the Dawsons wouldn't leave before got there. Somewhere in the distance, a tent waited, full of laughter and possibility. Reuben would shoot up playing cards with those B-B guns on chains, and throw those hard little balls until he had armfuls of stuffed animals. He would give his prizes to girls, who would be so happy they would want to kiss him again and again.

As long as the neighbors were not as forgetful as his family. Mrs. Dawson forgot that he had severe allergies and couldn't run through the field, but hopefully they would wait. The tractor could work. Reuben patted the John Deere like a cowboy with his trusty steed.

Reuben saw something on his left, a pile of movement just off of the path. He turned toward it, without meaning to, without really turning, more just looking.

The steady sway of the tractor's progress swung hard to the left and Reuben felt the lurch as the tractor progressed. Cornstalks slapped against his jeans, and Reuben tried not to breathe into the cloudy corn air that would surely choke him. A sound keened above the motor and Reuben breathed again, even though he didn't mean to.

A plangent and faraway sound.

Frozen moments ride on. He didn't see them in the field. He didn't think he saw them in the field. He certainly didn't mean to keep going with the tractor, but the thick air and the low light confused Reuben's eyes and Reuben's driving.

The tractor went over her before he knew what had happened.

Behind the tractor, two bodies tangled together, pale green in the moonlight. Another whining sound came, maybe from the motor. Maybe not. Reuben turned off the tractor and tried to regulate his ragged breaths. He tried to think of the color blue and will his heart to stop jumping around. He pulled his inhaler from his pocket and sucked desperately. With his eyes closed, he couldn't see behind him, couldn't see his brother's bare arms holding someone sobbing. Holding Aunt Rainy.

The trip back to the house took so long that Reuben worried that his parents would return from the concert before they got Aunt Rainy across the field.

"I'll drive her," Denny said. His chin and shoulders twitched. He raised his fingertips to the wound on the side of his head and quickly pulled them away.

Denny tried to lift Rainy's arm, maybe trying to help her up, but she made a threatening sound like the mutt Princess did when anyone approached her puppies.

"Dad doesn't let you drive the tractor," Reuben said. "Besides, I can't walk through the fields or I'll have an attack." He coughed.

Denny just nodded. His blond bangs were darkening with blood. Reuben didn't know if the blood belonged to his brother or his aunt.

"We have move you up to the tractor now," Denny said into Aunt Rainy's curled back.

"Just leave me here." She didn't look up. Denny shuddered.

"We're going to have to lift her, Reuben. Can you step down onto the runner and grab her arm?" Denny's voice was wet and vibrating.

With Denny's strong arms and Reuben's determination, they hauled Rainy onto Reuben's lap. On the first lift she barked a sound so sharp Denny almost dropped her. Reuben grabbed her arms to catch her. Denny lifted Aunt Rainy's hip up onto the tractor and her head fell to the side of Reuben's chest. She closed her eyes and her body became heavier and more fluid.

The hard plastic of Reuben's inhaler pressed into his thigh. He shifted beneath Aunt Rainy to move the plastic canister from under the weight of her left hip. She gave a small moan, and her skirt fell back from her moonlit flesh.

Reuben pulled the triangle of denim towards him, while steadying Aunt Rainy with his cool hand in the small of her sweaty back. Rainy pressed her eyes closed, and Denny stumbled along in the tractor's wake of sound.

Sunday,

Trim

(At the salon, a knife, oak-handle blade out of his sight, weighs against her hip. Clatters to floor. Hands stop.)

RADIO: On a hill far away stood an old rugged cross

(The knife rests amid the quiet chunks of graying hair. She returns knife to smock pocket. Comb lifts again.)

RADIO: 'Til my trophies at last I lay down

(Eyes meet in mirror, then his sink to her knife-shaped pocket. His hand runs across the cold, plastic cushion.)

SHE: Here.

(Reaches, pulls out not knife but stick, one that washed up, red, soft, with just a hint of a curve. Hands roll stick between thumb and forefinger, to the rhythm of gospel music, thick bark's soothing pattern, pressed into fingertips.)

SHE: It's gonna be a whistle. For the boy. The one went down the Greenbrier. For when he comes back.

RADIO: And exchange it someday for a crown.

(His eyes return to cloudy non-looking. He rises and brushes hair from his shoulders.)

SHE: On your way out, switch off the damned radio.

Dogs in

Country

Music

A green truck full of chickens took the wrong exit because the driver was bleary from the competing forces of spicy enchiladas—cheap rest stop eats—and ephedrine—cheap trucker's speed. The curve of the mountain road swung the back wheels into a blue-gray dog and tossed it three feet. Curling smoke from the retreating truck wound around the dog's owner, drinking in exhaust. A feather landed in her hair. Still attached by the umbilical of the leash, she stood frozen, watching her crushed pet twitch in front of her.

Another woman drove around the corner at a reasonable speed in a sensible family sedan. She saw a twisted back by the side of the road and thought of a statue she had seen in Italy once, in another lifetime. "The Rape of the Sabine Women"? "Uglino's Children," perhaps?

When one of her children's goldfish died (they really died constantly but luckily one looks just like another) this woman made her husband flush them. Yet now, she picked up a rock without hesitation and told the other woman to turn away. She lifted a red boulder the size of a man's head and dropped it firmly onto the dog's skull. The back leg made one more lazy circle and the animal was still.

"It's over now," she said.

The frozen woman began to sway, and the rock-heaving woman roped her arms around the shaking waist. Both blinked back separately conceived tears.

They stood like that for an indeterminable amount of time while a birthday cake wilted in the back of the family sedan.

Years later one of the women wrote a country-western song about that afternoon. The song was mournful with comic relief in the verse where she rhymed "bark" and "card shark." A man in a denim hat crooned the tune, because the woman had no singing voice to speak of. The other woman heard the song on the car radio and stopped to have a rapid four beers, her first in seven years. Such is the bittersweet potion of country music.

Small

Love

Story

If you counted it up, the couple had been on earth for less than a century. The woman slightly below fifty and the man slightly above. Their bodies betrayed their relative youth. The woman's hips were wide as wings, just not as symmetrical. Her internal organs, according to those pictures the doctor took, grew in strange directions, too. The man's left leg had retracted until it was the same shape and length as that of a seven-year-old boy, and his whole body twisted around it in a series of abstractly beautiful but highly impractical whorls. They had nine grown children, ten if you counted the one the woman had lost when a bearded mine foreman cut open the man's leg right in front of her.

"I've been praying." She touched her husband's hand.

"For more rain, perhaps?" he said, bridging his tongue across his remaining teeth.

"No. For our death, sweetheart." She smiled as she stirred the pot on the stove.

"Aren't you a wicked thing!" he said, and stood to fit his crooked body in the hollow between her huge buttocks. He held himself steady by gently digging four teeth into her soft shoulder for support. They stood like this often, mostly when she was cooking beneath the slanted slope of their ceiling. His bright eyes watched her pour a packet of rat poison into the venison stew. He guffawed a bit as the crystals dissolved.

She felt his smile in her shoulder.

The dinner was sweet as syrup and the two badly-proportioned people could not stop smiling at each other. They giggled like schoolgirls. After combing her white hair, the woman hefted her twisted husband in her pot-roast thick arms—a misshapen Pieta. They walked towards the creek.

Eventually, their three children who lived nearby came to investigate.

"They are gone."

"This is ridiculous."

"They must be here somewhere."

"I bet they finally did it. Ran off to see a city, or to the Grand Ole Opry. They always said they were going to run off. A second honeymoon or something."

"They are way too old and far too ugly to do such a thing."

"Shut your hole! You can only hope to be the same."

Choose Your Own Practical Husbandry and Haircut as an Expression of Appropriate Femininity, with Outside Influence from an Elderly Aunt

You wash your hair, leaving the conditioner on for at least three minutes, knowing you are wasting the hot water sloughing down from your shoulders. You throw on some clothes and check the mail. Someone out there sure wants you to refi! On a thick pink envelope sandwiched between credit card offers, you recognize your aunt's finely spun handwriting. You assume it's a note thanking you for coming to her husband's funeral last month, and making that sponge cake to boot.

The envelope lets out a sigh of perfume and Virginia Slims.

Dearest Niece,

Please read this letter twice and then tear it into pieces. Trust me. I have always loved your family and would not want to upset any of the delicate balances between relatives. Due to this love, I ask that you honor my first request. The one about tearing.

I was very happy to see you at the funeral. Thank you for paying respects to my Husband, who knew how to be a Husband to me but needed to be put out of his misery.

But you looked a maid servant.

I do not mean to be cruel. Only honest. Your hair is fly away and too unruly for a woman of your years. Your clothes were tableclothy. I tell you this to help.

Many women out there are desperate for Husbands. They would do Anything. The Divorced are the worst. The Divorced here will swoop on men who cannot perform any kind of manliness.

My Husband knew how much I loved my family and he knew I would do anything for them. This was Okay with my Husband. Each night before I went to bed I would wash and powder. Even between my legs. And brush my hair and my teeth. I am not embarrassed to say that my Husband turned to me for lovemaking even in his final year. Which was seventy-three.

You could make an effort and see the results for yourself. May I suggest most importantly that you cut your hair and try to be an Attractive Woman for a Husband?

Love Always,
    Your Aunt

Your bottom lip moves in strange ways, between your teeth. What does she want you to do with your hair? Get one of those old lady perms? And you take a bath every night, every single night, so any suggestion that you might be *unclean* is clearly preposterous. You even read that article about vinegar softening clothes, so you put vinegar in with the washing, making a clothes softener that's environmentally friendly.

Chemistry and husbandry.

You stand in front of the bathroom mirror and unhinge the clip holding your damp hair twisted against your head.

If you appreciate the strength of your body and ignore your aunt, who has been overly influenced by the histrionic covers of romance novels, turn to page 201.

If you stay longer in front of the mirror, being really honest with yourself to see if maybe the old bat has a point, turn to page 205.

If you go find a good bottle of wine even though it's not noon but who cares, turn to page 213.

Not bad. Eyes still smoke-gray. Not as many laugh-lines as some. You pluck a stray hair from your chin.

Women need to celebrate, find their jouissance.

You drop the towel to stand nude in the mirror and rub your hands down your flanks. Beautiful. Plenty soft. You find a few more hairs around your nipple, but that's to be expected.

If you want to celebrate your feminine beauty with a good bottle of wine, turn to page 213.

If you start to doubt yourself, turn to page 203.

If you're still not sure whether or not you need a new hairstyle, but aren't going to get your knickers in a twist over something so stupid, turn to page 205.

Patriarchy keeps women scraped clean. You've read far too many volumes of Julia Kristeva to fall for this. Surely Virginia Woolf wouldn't bother with the nonsense, wouldn't let it get her down.

Except for down to the bottom of the river. Ha ha. Get her down, get it?

When you digitized all the music, what happened to the Sinéad O'Connor?

If you find the Sinéad O'Connor and crank it, turn to page 209.

If you wonder what happened to that girl you made out with in college, get out the photos and turn to page 211.

If you stop pretending you don't want the wine, turn to page 213.

Not by the hair of my chinny-chin-chin.

Maybe a new hairstyle and some highlights would refresh. Maybe it's time to reinvent yourself. Your aunt means well and wants you to be happy. Why not take a widow's best wishes for the gift that they are?

You pull your hair up into a pageboy, into a soccer-mom bob. No-ethnicity-Middle-America stares back. You look at yourself until your eyes blur and you refocus on the reflection beside your face, a framed image of Hildegard of Bingen that your college friend gave you years ago.

An anchoress doesn't give a shit. An anchoress offers the patriarchy but a peephole. An anchoress doesn't care about the husbandry because her chemistry is purely spiritual.

If wine would improve this crapshow of a morning, turn to page 213.

If you think Sinéad O'Connor is a contemporary anchoress, dust off your college music collection and turn to page 209.

If you reject the lonely anchoress route because the type of martyr you'd prefer involves motherhood, take a deep breath and turn to page 207.

You need to refocus on the fact that you still want to have kids someday. If you chase wild notions down primrose paths then you'll never be a mother. Although, truth be told, Sylvia Plath struggled with the impositions and noise of mothering.

Guess how that worked out for her, for the bottle of milk, for Anne Sexton's jealousy so far away? No Anne or Sylvia now, not for you.

You let down your hair and think about children. Miracles really. Expensive miracles who cannot take care of themselves and someday resent you.

Much of parenting is pretending, listening to boring stories and slogging through the drudgery, doing laundry. A natural fit for women, who costume themselves and pretend to be what they wear. Mothering is all about putting on a good front, playing the appropriate role. You acted in college. You could do it.

You would choose gender-neutral names and put no kind of restrictions on boy-toy or girl-toy. You know the ropes and would never allow a princess movie except for that one that you watched with her back in the day, laughing and clutching.

Your aunt herself has the hair of defeat, the hair of the Midwest, the hair that represents the helmet of shame, of submissions, of television shows with laugh tracks.

If you miss your sweet friend, the one from college, take a trip down memory lane and turn to page 211.

If you call your aunt to get her advice, you should have a drink first so turn to page 213.

If you realize that thinking about reproducing is the wrong way to cheer up, grab a bottle of wine and turn to page 213.

Sinéad O'Connor knows that female hair is just another tool of oppression. You could go full Sinéad, and get rid of the expectations and responsibilities of keeping a head of hair in a certain configuration. And yet. A smooth scalp would draw attention to the darkening fuzz on your upper lip, or that near-pube that grows right in the hollow of your cheek.

Plus, Sinéad lost her children, lost everything. That has to do with the Irish patriarchy and the lack of mental health services, but maybe the hair didn't help. Maybe the hair never helps, whether you take it or you leave it.

If you raise a glass to Sinéad for fighting the good fight, turn it up and turn to page 213.

If you worry that Sinéad won't solve it but nothing else will either, calm yourself and turn to page 213.

If you want to go back in time, kiss your friend's softness again, shave your head and make all these decisions without hair, but the relentless progression makes that impossible, embrace the possible on page 213.

You couldn't go further than you went then, when you were the girl in the pictures. The photos show you laughing, on the fire escape, in that costume. You don't remember really laughing like that, but you remember your friend, on your left, the one with the soft lips, dark eyes and extensive book collection. The particular chemistry of your evenings spent arguing about post-structuralism went beyond hairstyle into the realm of pure joy. Whatever happened to her? Why haven't you talked to her in all these years?

If thinking about her makes you want to listen to the Sinéad O'Conner CD you always listened to together, turn to page 209.

If regrets about your life choices overwhelm, turn to page 213.

You pull the wine from the cabinet and open it, the wine you were saving for something special. It's been a few years now, but special doesn't come around as often as it used to. You feel like breaking the bottle over your own head, like you are the boob shot on the prow of a boat, but you don't, you just swallow long and laugh at the idea of being a topless statue lashed to boat—as if that would ever bring good luck!

If you make an appointment at a high-end salon, turn to page 239.

On second thought, forget that. High-end salons are patriarchal garbage. Seriously. Forget it. Who cares? Turn to page 215.

When you finish the wine, you call your aunt. Maybe you haven't just finished the one bottle, but have also started another. You've finished something. Hard to tell.

You chat and she unwinds a long story about her first husband and a suspicious bottle of perfume. You talk about making out with your best friend in college. You're not sure you actually called your aunt. You might have called someone else altogether. Sinéad sings loud (LOUD) about what would be a good idea.

You're pretty sure the phone call's over, or at least that you can no longer find the phone. You stand in front of the mirror. You have trouble considering your hair with so many distractions, so you take off the stupid clothes you're wearing.

It's not even hair anymore. This shit is snakes.

ACKNOWLEDGMENTS

Fantastic people make fictions a reality. Heather Preusser keeps all those writing dates, and Jeannie O'Toole makes me a part of her amazing family. So many offer unflagging support: Sue and Jeb Bobbin, Debbie and Bob Letter, Michelle Bredbenner, Barbara Leffler, Gary Drescher, Barbara Lemon, Patty Kelly, Galen Gaardner, Suzanne Frost, Brian Rauscher, Justin Wheeler, Stacy Berg, Joe Howard, Lauren Sessions, Karen Amidon, Bob Hettmansperger, Jeanne Bayerl, Kanesha Baynard, Becky Trifillis, Courtney Hanna-McNamara, Yulissa Segura, Brett Hill, Michele Bartley, Melanie Kiehl, and Laura Smith Johnson. Victoria Barrett reads so carefully and cares. As the world's best librarians, Katy McNicol and Sheena Kelly keep the dream going. Sages Rachel Basch, Eugenia Kim, and Susan Muaddi Durraj inspire. The booziest book club in the world reads above and beyond—Cathy, Jane, Wendy, Brian, Nicole, Val, Tara. My lovely kids accept their distracted parent and Bobby is absolutely everything (and then some). Thank you.

ABOUT THE AUTHOR

Kristie Betts Letter's writing has been featured in *The Massachusetts Review*, *The North Dakota Quarterly*, *Washington Square*, *Passages North*, *Pangolin Papers*, and *The Southern Humanities Review*, and has been honored by Best American Short Fictions, the Tom Howard Writing Awards, and Terrain Environmental Writing Awards. Her poetry collection *Under-Worldly* (Editorial L'Aleph 2017) also examines what lies beneath with what *Cowboy Jamboree* describes as "fantastic images of the subterranean grit." When not writing, she encourages high school students to write and explores old mining towns with her family in Colorado.

CPSIA information can be obtained
at www.ICGtesting.com
Printed in the USA
JSHW021121311019
2167JS00001B/1